"Ed. That's the lam

Gaia raised her hea   get a better look at him. He opene his eyes and turned back to her. "What are you talking about? That's brilliant fake snoring."

"You sound like a goat clearing his throat."

"Yeah, well. . ."

Gaia examined the bump on his head, touching her index finger gently to the bruise. "Does it hurt?"

"It kills," he said.

"I'll go get you some ice." Gaia got one foot off the side of the bed before Ed grasped her arm.

"Don't go," he said quietly. "Stay here, okay?"

Don't miss any books in this thrilling series:

FEARLESS™

Available from SIMON PULSE

FEARLESS™

TWINS

FRANCINE PASCAL

SIMON PULSE
New York   London   Toronto   Sydney   Singapore

To Hilary Bloom

First Simon Pulse edition January 2002

Text copyright © 2002 by Francine Pascal

Cover copyright © 2002 by 17th Street Productions, an Alloy, Inc. company.

SIMON PULSE
An imprint of Simon & Schuster Children's Publishing Division
1230 Avenue of the Americas, New York, NY 10020

Produced by 17th Street Productions,
an Alloy, Inc. company
151 West 26th Street
New York, NY 10001

Printed in the United States of America
10 9 8 7 6 5 4 3 2 1

Library of Congress Control Number: 2001098568
ISBN: 0-7434-4397-7

I've never told anyone this before, but for the first five years of my life—before the specialists could figure out what the hell was wrong with me—my parents considered the possibility that I might be mentally challenged. You know, "slow." See, I kept doing all these things that seemed extraordinarily stupid, and my parents couldn't figure out why. My mother had been top of her class at the university in Moscow. My father tested at the genius level. It wouldn't make sense for their only child to be a moron.

Of course, certain signs pointed to the fact that I was smarter than I acted. I picked up languages really quickly; I was doing algebra when most girls are debating whether or not to give up playing with dolls. It was my behavior that baffled them. Like when I was four, they took me to this hotel in Los Angeles. There was an Olympic-size swimming pool. I took one look at it, and then I dove headfirst into the deep end. I didn't have the faintest inkling how to swim.

Needless to say, I almost drowned. But that wasn't the disturbing part. The problem was, I dove right back into the deep end the next day. And the next. I'll never forget the look on my father's face every time he fished me out of the warm turquoise water and wagged his long finger in my face with anxious fury. "What is the matter with you?" he kept yelling.

I couldn't answer him. I didn't know.

There were a lot of incidents like that: diving into giant swimming pools, running past the shark warnings into the ocean, walking into traffic, pedaling my tricycle for six miles with no idea how to get back home. . . .

It wasn't until the Agency ran some tests on me that we all discovered that I was missing that pesky little fear gene. Oh, happy day! My ludicrous behavior could finally be explained.

I wasn't stupid. I was fearless.

They'd just confused the two, which, when you think about it, makes perfect sense. I understood what I was doing; I just didn't care about the consequences. So I kept making bad decisions. My ability to reason hadn't caught up with my instincts yet.

And that's really the problem. When you're fearless and you're only acting on instinct. . . you can do some pretty stupid things. I mean, think about it. How can you make the right choice when you don't fear the consequences of the wrong one? How can you even tell the difference between right and wrong, between sensible and idiotic?

Yes, there is a point I'm getting to here.

Three minutes ago I had to make a choice. A choice based entirely on instinct. Josh Kendall and Loki's thugs were

coming at me. (How Josh could
have been there, given that I'd
just seen him shot in the head a
few hours earlier, is another
story entirely—one I have yet to
figure out and one that is simply
too twisted and inexplicable for
me to deal with right now. So I
will stick to what I understand.)
I was basically cornered. And
then a car pulled up to the curb
and a man opened the back door,
begging me to jump into the car
with him, where I'd be safe.

I looked at his face, and I
had two seconds to decide. . . .
Was that man my father or my
uncle? There was no time for
quizzes or close consideration.
No time to reason. I looked deep
in his eyes, and my gut told me
that he was my father. So I got
in the car, and we took off down
the street.

But I just don't know.

I mean, someone actually capable of experiencing fear would
know better than I would. Did I
make the right choice or not?

Have my instincts improved with age, or did I just dive into the deep end again? Here I was, sitting in the backseat of the car with my father, and the same thought kept running through my head over and over again:

I should be afraid. I really wish I were afraid right now.

She wanted
to be
shouting,
but her
body was no
longer **eyes**
capable of
responding
to her
demands.

THE CHAOS AND CONFUSION ENDED

A Simple Hug

so suddenly. Gaia couldn't adapt to the serene white noise that took its place. Moments ago her world had been utter cacophony: the stomps of the enemy closing in on her, the screech of burning rubber tires on asphalt, the insistent voice of her father (or her uncle) shouting for her to get in the car. Now it was nothing but the cool, sterile interior of a black Mercedes.

But the silence made no difference. Gaia's head was still pounding—her confused thoughts wailing like a jumbo jet in a dizzying tailspin.

She glanced out the window. She hadn't even noticed they were on FDR Drive. The East River ran just beside the highway, but it was too dark to see by night, especially through the tinted window. The starless sky was as black as the water. Gaia pressed a button to open the window, allowing the dark glass to slide all the way down into the door. Then she leaned forward and closed her eyes, letting the wind pummel her face and eyelids. It roared thunderously in her ears. She hoped to numb her senses, to sandblast all the horrors of the last twenty-four hours. Maybe the harsh wind could just strip her away layer by layer until she could no longer feel that rotten crust of guilt and disappointment that was hardening around her like a shell. . . .

Yeah, right. *The Winds of Change.* When was the last time the wind had actually changed anything?

Nothing could alter the facts. Sam was dead. It was still basically her fault. And Ed was drifting farther away with every revolution of the car's wheels. If she'd made it into his building before the ambush, she would have asked him to leave with her. Tonight. Immediately. Not to go anyplace specific, but just to *go.* Away from where they were. Not as boyfriend and girlfriend, but not exactly just friends. Just as. . . whatever they were. Or whatever they might become.

It doesn't matter now, she told herself. That imaginary future had been yanked out from under her just as quickly as she'd conjured it up. It was just another dead issue to be tossed into the fire along with all of her other short-lived pipe dreams and useless bursts of optimism. Only her father knew where she was going now. And that was the problem.

He was sitting right beside her, his hands tightly on the wheel, and she had no idea what to say. In the past twenty-four hours she'd formed every conceivable opinion of him, directed every possible feeling toward him—from unadulterated hatred to desperate concern to utter confusion. His identity had changed in Gaia's mind literally from hour to hour, depending on which lies Loki was feeding her. He'd gone from neglectful father to murder suspect to kidnapper to noble parent. . . . In fact, her perceptions had shifted so many times, she found she could barely trust any opinions or feelings. Even the good ones. She could hardly even bring herself to look at him.

But the longer she avoided him, the more questions she found piling up in her head. Sam was dead, but did her father know anything else? Or about Josh, who should have been dead himself but had somehow avoided giving Gaia the satisfaction? Maybe her father had been there when it happened—when Loki and Josh put an end to Sam's innocent life. Was anyone else there for Sam? Did anyone try to help him? Did he die completely alone?

Suddenly the image of Sam dropping to his knees from a gunshot darted through Gaia's mind. Her body tensed. She couldn't think about it. The guilt was simply too overwhelming. She forced herself to shake it off by leaning farther out the window. She opened her mouth as the wind scraped away at her lips and her throat. She couldn't ask her father about Sam. Not yet. It was still too fresh, too painful.

But she at least needed to know about her uncle. No one in that Chelsea loft had been able to tell her father and uncle apart—not George, not a gang of agents, not even Gaia herself. One of them had escaped, and one of them had been captured. And if her father was indeed driving, then her uncle—the man she now knew was Loki—was the one they'd cuffed and sent back to jail.

"Where are we going?" she asked finally.

He glanced at her, a faint smile forming in the corner of his mouth. "Just be glad we made it, sweetheart," he said. Slices of light flashed across his shadowy face from the passing streetlamps. "Don't worry. I'm taking you someplace safe."

"Yeah, but where?" Gaia persisted. This was no time for cryptic answers. He should know that.

His smile grew larger and more relaxed. "Don't worry," he assured her. He eased up on the gas as they approached Houston Street, pulling off the highway to an abandoned lot. The car lurched to an abrupt halt. He turned to face her. "We're home free, sweetheart. Free of all of it now. Come here."

He inched closer, opening his arms to her and offering an embrace.

For no reason that Gaia could understand, the gesture made her skin crawl. She stared into his eyes. He *was* her father; she was certain of it. So what was the problem? Had their distance done this much damage? Was her ability to trust him so bruised and battered that the thought of a simple hug had actually come to disgust her? A hug from her dad used to be one of the only three things that could actually cheer her up—the other two being a hug from her mom and chocolate cheesecake. But here was blatant and disheartening proof that her childhood was over. The outstretched arms made her stiff and numb and uneasy.

Still, she knew that she had to respond in kind. They had to start rebuilding their mess of a relationship.

Gaia allowed him to take her in his arms. But a nebulous black thought began to stir in some very remote region of her brain—a thought that was unformed but deeply foreboding. She felt his chin nestled in her neck. His arms were oddly serpentine, sliding across her back and locking her against him. Every part of her wanted to break free from his embrace. The repulsion was palpable. It was almost as if there were a faint inaudible voice buried in her head, trying to dig its way out, trying to tell her something. Her subconscious was sending her images—speaking to her in visual code. She saw herself at four years old, flailing helplessly at the bottom of that sun-drenched, light blue swimming pool. She saw herself as a kindergartner, making a beeline for the turbulent ocean, completely ignoring the huge sign that warned of shark-infested waters.

Finally her inner voice clawed its way to the surface.

You're not certain at all, it whispered. *You've made a mistake.*

Gaia quickly moved to extricate herself—but felt a sharp stinging prick to her arm. "Ow," she hissed. She slapped the spot reflexively. But there was no mosquito or horsefly. As she leaned back, she caught a glimpse of something clasped between his thumb and forefinger: a long syringe. Her gaze darted to his eyes. One glance confirmed what her subconscious had been trying to tell her all this time. Those weren't her father's eyes. And it wasn't her father's embrace that had repulsed her.

Loki had set a trap. And Gaia had—fearlessly— jumped right in.

"I'm so sorry, Gaia," he said. "I truly am. I hate having to deceive you." He placed a cap over the syringe and tucked it back in the pocket of his overcoat.

Gaia shook her head. She could only hear him out of her right ear. The left ear was clogged with static. A second later the right ear started closing up as well. Her uncle was beginning to look two-dimensional, as if he were blending into the black background of the car's interior.

"Stop the car," Gaia shouted.

Only. . . she wasn't shouting. She wanted to be shouting, but her body was no longer capable of responding to her demands. "Stop the car," she repeated. The words were no more than a whisper. Her lips had gone numb, as had the rest of her face.

"It's just a sedative," Loki said gently, leaning toward her again. "I'm so sorry, Gaia, but I had no choice. I know how little you trust me now, and I had to get you away from Tom somehow. Just rest now, sweetheart. When you wake up, you'll be safe, and I'll explain everything."

"Stop. . . ," Gaia began again, but she was unable to complete the sentence. She focused every ounce of energy on her eyelids. She had to keep them open, no matter how heavy they might feel. She was a fighter. She wouldn't lose consciousness. She couldn't. Her body fell helplessly back against the seat.

Stay awake, Gaia! she screamed silently. *Fight it.*

This sensation was similar to the blackouts that always followed her fights. It was more aggressive. Insistent. Her iron will crumbled even as she pleaded with her body to attack, to pounce. . . to hurl her uncle's body through the window. But she could hardly make herself blink.

"I know you don't believe me," he said. He ran a hand gently down her paralyzed cheek. "I swear this is all for your own good. This is all because I love you. I'll prove it to you, Gaia. Just have patience."

The light dimmed. He was rapidly disappearing— his face now little more than a silhouette. Gaia's eyelids fluttered. It had a `nauseating strobe effect` on what was left of her vision.

Stay awake, she screamed at herself again. *Stay. . .* But before she could complete the thought, her consciousness faded completely.

WAITING FOR GAIA HAD BEGUN TO

make Ed Fargo feel like he'd been
beamed into one of those insane-
asylum movies. *Ed, Interrupted.* So
he'd forced himself out on another
night walk. But of course, that only
made him feel worse. Given that
Gaia could be beaten up and lying
in any alley or gutter, it didn't really
help to take a leisurely tour of alleys
and gutters—which, at three in the

The Obvious Maybe

morning, pretty much stood out as the defining features of downtown New York City.

About eight blocks into the walk, Ed suddenly
realized that he was being an idiot.
What the hell was he doing eight blocks from home?
Gaia might be collapsing at his door at this very second—just as she had the night before. And here he
was out, for an evening stroll. He quickly reversed
himself and started crutching back toward his building as fast possible, nearly pole vaulting across the
sidewalk. . . looking very much like just another loony
out on the streets in the middle of the night.

He never should have let her go after Sam by herself. That had been his first mistake. (Well, not really—
it had actually been about his thousandth mistake in
the past forty-eight hours.) But true to Amazonian
form, Gaia had insisted that she handle everything on

her own. Since then he'd been doing everything in his power to maintain a sense of humor and stave off panic, but he couldn't. Not anymore. Sleep deprivation alone was tearing him to shreds.

She'd left him more than eight hours ago. He hadn't heard one word from her since. He'd run through stacks and stacks of maybes in his head. Maybe she never found her uncle or her father and she'd finally forced herself to skip town. Maybe she found Sam and rescued him and they'd run off together for a life of wild romance on some Caribbean island. Maybe the whole Sam kidnapping was a hoax or a practical joke or something and now she and Sam and her father and her uncle were laughing about the whole thing over a couple of cold ones. . . .

Each maybe had to be more ludicrous than the last. It had to be crazy enough to keep Ed's mind occupied; otherwise he would have to consider the most obvious maybe. The maybe he'd been dreading and avoiding for the last three hours. The maybe he had to avoid at all costs. `Allowing it to enter his mind would be like voluntarily submitting himself to Chinese water torture.` He'd just finally confessed to being completely in love with her—and she'd *promised* him that she would be back. They still had a conversation to finish. Ed had to believe that Gaia kept every one of her promises. Of course. He knew she did.

But that thought only served to bring Ed right back to the worst-case scenario.

Given that Gaia kept all her promises, given that only a sadist would let Ed pour his guts out, then leave him hanging without a word. . . there was no way her disappearance could have been by choice. None at all.

By the time he reached the lobby, Ed was drenched in sweat. He practically fell into the elevator, panting until it opened on his floor. Then he dashed to the apartment. He left the key in the lock as he swung open the door.

"Gaia?" he called out hopefully. "Gaia, are you here?"

Silence.

Ed paused in the middle of his living room. She wasn't here. He had no idea what to do. He should call someone—the cops, Heather, even his parents upstate (wherever the hell they were). But all he could do was stand there in the oppressive and ugly quiet. The apartment had never felt so empty. He'd always loved having the place to himself, but now that Gaia had lived with him for a day, it felt wrong without her. As far as Ed was concerned, it had already become her home, too.

And he was getting the distinct feeling that she wouldn't be coming home.

The most obvious maybe. . . The thought of it began weighing him down, crushing him toward the floor like excess gravity, causing his shaky legs to ache and nearly buckle from the pressure. All the wishes and fantasies and complicated scenarios faded away. There was really only one thought that remained.

Just please be alive, he prayed silently.

He could survive if she didn't love him the way he loved her. He could survive if she ran off with Sam. He could even somehow survive if he never saw her again. Barely—as long as he knew she was all right. But if Gaia hadn't survived, then neither could he. It was as simple as that.

WHITE CEILING. BRIGHT LIGHT.

Contradictory Purposes

The room darted in and out of focus like a television on the fritz. As she crept back into consciousness, Gaia tried to gather as many visual details as possible. But she could still only keep her eyes open for a few seconds at a time. Her head was lolling. It felt like it had been filled with rubber cement and left to dry. The need for sleep was more powerful than any other force on earth. She was sitting somewhere. . . .

Flowered vase. Silver candlestick holders. Medical

tray. Latex gloves. The random images weren't adding up. *Moroccan rug. Mahogany desk. Scalpels. Syringes. Two microscopes.* Was she in a medical lab or a living room? Or was she still asleep?

She tried to massage her temples. She couldn't move her hands. Once again she forced her eyes to flutter open—and even though the dry, stinging retinas begged to be tucked back under the lids, she fought back. Gradually her vision adjusted to the blinding sunlight from the windows behind her. Her paralyzed hands swam into focus. No. . . they weren't paralyzed. They were restrained, strapped firmly to the arms of her chair with two buckles. Her feet were restrained, too, ankles bound against the front legs of her chair. She used what little strength she had to try to wrench her wrists free of the restraints, but it was pointless. Her resistance only served to cut off the circulation, turning her flesh different shades of purple and crimson.

She was trapped.

Any remotely normal person would be terrified at this point. Strapped down. Vulnerable to anything and everything that Loki had in mind—grotesque genetic experiments, mutilation, torture. She might as well have been blindfolded, given a cigarette, and placed in front of the firing line. She was, for all intents and purposes, dead. Without fear to occupy her mind, however, all

Gaia could feel was sickeningly angry. And groggy. And most of all, foolish.

She'd gathered such a vast wealth of knowledge in her short life. She could match wits with experts on any number of topics—calculus, chaos theory, Eastern European history, molecular biology. . . but her instincts? Without fear to inform her decisions, her instincts were still those of a goddamn four-year-old. She could have taken on Josh and those goons. She could have taken them all on. Why the hell had she gotten in that car? Why couldn't she *see* that it was Loki and not her father? Why—

The sound of a turning doorknob put her questions on hold.

Gaia raised her bleary eyes, watching as her uncle stepped quietly into the room, like a concerned father trying not to wake his baby. She wondered for a moment just how deeply deranged he might be. His look of concern was repulsive. But the moment he saw her, his expression shifted. His eyes narrowed. His lips tensed into a livid scowl. He ducked his head back behind the door and spat out some inaudible complaint.

"Now!" he finished. "Get in here now!"

Two faceless thugs—as nondescript and familiar as every other she'd encountered—rushed into the room and dropped to their knees directly in front of her.

"Get them off," Loki barked. "I never said to use restraints." He turned to Gaia. "I'm so sorry," he murmured gently. His ability to completely change his demeanor from one moment to the next was disturbing, fascinating. But this was hardly the time to indulge in a psychological profile. She had to size up the situation and figure a way out of it.

Her senses were still slightly numb, but she could feel the thugs' thick, calloused fingers digging into her skin as they tugged at her restraints and unbuckled them. Finally the blood flowed freely through her wrists. Strength surged back into her limbs. Yes, she was coming out of it now—all the while taking mental notes for a potential escape. The men untying her were armed with nine-millimeter pistols. Not a surprise.

Gaia turned back toward her uncle and studied his eyes suspiciously. She couldn't help but wonder if Loki hadn't prearranged this little episode with the restraints. It did, after all, seem to serve Loki's two very contradictory purposes perfectly. He could present himself as the caring father figure, insisting that they "free" his niece. That would demonstrate his "compassion." But without ever openly threatening her, he could also send a very clear message: she was free to run, but there was no point in trying to escape.

She'd begun to
feel like a hollow
plastic Ping-Pong
ball, incessantly

emotional

bounced,
batted, **lexicon**
and spiked back
and forth
between them.

GAIA FELT LIKE THE ROOM WAS slanting on its axis, her entire perception dipping into a forty-five-degree angle and then snapping back upright like a seesaw. She was ninety-eight percent sure that she was awake, but anything was possible. She needed to sharpen her focus and clear out the cobwebs in her head.

The Same Phrase

Her weakness and physical exhaustion were beyond her control, but physical force wasn't how Loki did most of his damage. It was mental strength she would need if she wanted to survive this unfortunate tête-à-tête. She had to go on the offensive before Loki found some way to psychologically corner her.

"You're not making any sense," she croaked, clearing her throat to sound less meek and helpless. "If you want to 'give me my life back,' then call off the firing squad and let me go."

"Gaia," Loki began, his voice tinged with rancid sweetness. "You simply don't understand—"

"What's there to understand?" she snapped. A jittery anger was bubbling up from her sternum and taking over. "I understand that any kind of life I had, you've stomped out completely. You killed my mother, you tried to kill my father, and now you've killed Sam. So exactly what part of my life are you planning to give back?" Her throat was raw and burning. (Maybe it was from straining to raise her voice, or maybe it was just the acid erupting in her stomach and shooting up through her esophagus.)

"Not *me*, Gaia," her uncle insisted, kneeling before her, eye to eye. "*I'm* not the one who did those things. Loki's got you completely confused—"

"No!" Gaia shouted. It came out far more desperate and defensive than she had planned, but she couldn't possibly endure this game again—the never-ending game of oppositional accusations being hurled back and forth between her father and her uncle. Both had proclaimed their innocence so many times, insisting that the other was the true Loki. She'd begun to feel like a hollow plastic Ping-Pong ball, incessantly bounced, batted, and spiked back and forth between them. But her uncle didn't seem to understand that the game was over. It had ended in his loft hours earlier.

"I know now," she said, trying valiantly to stare him down, hoping she might somehow be able to spit some of that stomach acid directly into his face. "You may have drugged me, but do you think I've totally forgotten all of last night?"

"What are you talking about?" He stared wide-eyed at Gaia as if *she* were somehow the crazy one in the room.

"God, don't you ever stop?" She groaned. "We were

all in the same room, *Loki*. I watched you aim a gun at my father's face and tell him you wanted him dead. I watched you fire a bullet through Josh Kendall's head. And somehow Josh isn't dead. Maybe you want to explain that, too—"

"You're so wrong. That boy wasn't talking to me; he was talking to your father. He worked for your father. And that boy had a gun, Gaia—he was pulling another gun from behind his back. He was going to kill you. I had to shoot him before he shot you. I had no choice."

"Stop it," Gaia insisted, finding the strength in her legs to rise from her chair. She wobbled away from her uncle's eerily convincing eyes and steadied herself by the window. "I know the truth now. I know it for myself, not from any of the bull the two of you have hurled at me. I know, Loki."

"Please don't call me by that hideous name," he snapped. He rose to his feet and glared at her. "You don't know anything."

He looked so offended and emotionally wounded, his expression bordered on angry. Gaia turned to the window, shielding her eyes from the harsh sunlight. But she was starting to feel more like herself. Her strength was returning in minuscule increments. Maybe she could at least place herself geographically. Maybe there was a deep enough ledge to climb onto or a fire escape. Maybe they were only a few stories up.

The sun-blurred landscape shifted into view. She stifled a sigh of disappointment. Not only was there no ledge or fire escape, but she was high above the vast downtown skyline. This room, this apartment or whatever it was, must be at least twenty stories up.

"I meant every word I said to your father," her uncle continued from behind her as he closed in. "I did want him dead. That is true. Because he's killed or mangled everything I love. He lives for no other reason than to damage and destroy people. And then he places the blame on *me*. Can you imagine the kind of anger that has bred in me? Can you imagine the depths of resentment—"

"Can you imagine how much I want you to shut up?" she interrupted as she dropped her forehead against the hot windowpane.

Oliver slammed his hand on the window, sending a wicked vibration through her skull and down her spine. She probably would have jumped from the shock of it `if shock were part of her emotional lexicon`. He clamped his hand on her shoulder and turned her toward him so that they were face-to-face—practically nose-to-nose.

"Don't belittle this," he snapped. "Don't belittle what he's done to me. And to your mother, and to Sam Moon. Don't belittle what he's done to you."

For the slightest millisecond Gaia felt a wave of belief rush over her like a bolt of electricity. His eyes were so unquestionably sincere. But there was no way. There was no way he was telling the truth. She was through listening to either one of them. She reminded herself of that ten times over. *You're half awake. You're trapped, and you're at rock bottom here. Close your ears. Ward him off. Keep him away.*

"Move back," she ordered, staring into his eyes with cold defiance. He seemed confounded by her warning, so she clarified it for him. "Take. . . a step. . . back."

He stared at her for two full seconds and then honored her request.

"I know what you're doing," she said. "I've seen the CD already. I mean, for chrissake, I can see we're in a medical lab. This must be part two of Clofaze, right?"

His eyes gave nothing away. His expression was compassionate but blank. Gaia went on, anyway.

"I know all about your plan," she said. "Clofaze. My father gave me a copy of the disk. So the way I see it, part one was to capture me. Well, congratulations, you've done that brilliantly. So what's part two? I'm not up on the latest advances in cloning. That's where your dementia comes in."

He gazed at her in silence. A hint of sadness revealed itself in the corners of his eyes.

"I want to show you something," he said, walking away from her to the large mahogany desk by the adjacent window. He took a set of small silver keys from his shirt pocket, selecting one and unlocking the roll-top cover of the desk. He pulled out a thick, weathered black binder and flipped it open. "Come here."

Gaia stood her ground at the window.

"Gaia"—he beckoned—"this *Clofaze* is a total fiction concocted by your father. Now, I could stand here and try to refute all his nonsense and give you the real story, but I know you're sick to death of hearing us try to convince you what's true and what's not. If you want to know the truth, the *real* truth—it's right here. In this book. You can stop listening to either one of us, and you can see it for yourself."

Gaia glanced at the black binder.

The book was surely filled with more lies. But she couldn't fight her curiosity. Of course she wanted to see what was in that binder. Who on this planet wouldn't? And she realized something, too. The moment he'd opened it, some part of her already believed that whatever was inside it was true.

All at once Gaia found herself standing next to her uncle at the desk, staring down hungrily at the aging color photos inside. No matter how much she yearned to live in the present moment and focus on the future, she was still far too obsessed with all the unanswered questions from her past. She couldn't begin to count the number of hours she'd spent staring at that one photograph hanging by the stairs of George Niven's town house—the picture of her family standing in front of their house in the Berkshires, before her mother had been killed. Before her father had abandoned her. Before her life had turned into. . . well, *this*.

Gaia had stared at that picture so many times, searching the faces of its subjects deeper and deeper until all she could see were the individual grains of the photo. Her photographic memory could recall facts and figures and images impeccably, but feelings? Intentions? Relationships? Those were what she'd always searched for in the picture. Why had her father held her and not her mother? Why did her father's face seem so kind but somehow—somewhere around the eyes and the forehead—troubled? And why did Gaia seem so oblivious to all those questions, just sitting there, draped in her father's arms, flashing that oversized, clueless grin?

"Do you recognize him?" Oliver asked, pointing his finger at the young man's face in the picture on the right-hand page. "He's not me, Gaia. I know you know that."

It was true. She might have trouble telling them apart now, but this picture was from a very long time ago, and her childhood memories of her father's face were perfect and indelible. She'd gazed at him adoringly way too many times to ever mistake him for anyone else. The man in the picture was her father.

He was standing with three other far too serious-looking men in white coats, the four of them posed uncomfortably for a picture that appeared to be solely for the purpose of documentation. Gaia became so fascinated with her father's youthful features, she neglected at first to look farther down on the photo. The four men weren't alone. They were all hovering over a metal rolling table draped with a large white sterile pad. And curled up on that table, taking up barely a foot and a half of space, was a small baby—no older than six months. Gaia looked at the bottom of the photo, where there were a few words stamped in red ink.

FILE #74-JL37 PROJECT INTREPID 1983

Then written by hand in the bottom corner, it read:

SUBJECT AT FIVE MONTHS, TWENTY DAYS

"No one in the Agency was supposed to have access to this file," Oliver said, flipping slowly through the pages and shaking his head with righteous disapproval. "This was a covert operation—cloaked from all the other agents. When I got hold of it and found out what Tom was doing to you. . . that was my last day at the Agency. I was disillusioned and disgusted. Certainly with the Agency, but most of all with my brother. It was the first time I realized what was happening to him."

Gaia could feel a toxic dread building inside her as she flipped quickly through the documents and photos. The first photo might have been of her father, but every other photo was of her—practicing martial arts from her earliest years all the way through her most recent street fights in Washington Square Park. She was too tense and frazzled to focus well on the details of the seemingly endless documents, but the same phrase kept appearing in bold letters within the extensive observations. Again and again she would read it.

0% FEAR FACTOR—SERUM EFFECTIVE

The last photo was a picture of her fighting off Josh and his thugs. It had obviously been taken through the window of Sam's dorm room. There was a handwritten subtitle at the bottom:

SUBJECT AT SEVENTEEN YEARS, SIX MONTHS, TEN DAYS

"My source has been sending me the additions to the file for seventeen years," Oliver said. "Your whole life."

Gaia turned back to the group photo with her father. "What is this?" she murmured, mostly to herself.

Oliver stared at the binder. "This. . . ," he uttered, staring regretfully at the binder. "This is what your father has done to you."

HE WAS STILL SO GODDAMN SEXY.

Small Tears

Even after everything they'd been through, after all of it was over and done with, Heather still found herself hesitating at the door to MacGregor's class and watching Ed Fargo through the window.

Apparently they'd both arrived at school a full fifteen minutes before first period.

She traced the lines of his shadowed profile set against the shaft of sunlight pouring through the classroom window. There was still something about the contrast of his chin and his scruffy dark brown hair. . . all the force of a man, mixed with the freedom of a teenage boy. . . .

Wait a second.

Heather leaned closer to the door's window to confirm what she thought she saw. And yes, she was right. That was a tear streaming slowly from his left eye as he stared blankly out the window. She snapped out of her pointless, voyeuristic gaze and stepped into the otherwise empty classroom.

"Ed?" she whispered gently. "Are you okay?"

Ed jumped. He threw her a crooked fake smile. "Hey. What's up?"

"Nothing," Heather answered, dragging another chair next to his and leaning toward him. She examined his face further in the awkward silence. She could think of no tactful way to ask the question, so she just came out with it. "Were you crying?"

"No," Ed replied quickly. He twisted his head back toward the window.

Heather knew why there was so much pain in his eyes. She was just avoiding the obvious. *Gaia Moore.* Only Gaia could elicit that kind of raw emotion from Ed at this point, and that fact left Heather with a muddle of conflicting thoughts too complicated to dissect.

She knew that Gaia was knee-deep in some kind of crisis, although she didn't totally understand the situation. Something to do with Gaia's father and Sam. That was about as much as she knew. But nonetheless, just the day before, Heather had decided to help Gaia with her crisis—to reach out to her in spite of all the prior hatred.

Someone was apparently stalking Gaia, and as insane as it might have been, Heather had agreed to help her carry out a little antistalker plan. Heather, along with all of her friends, had actually found the courage to dress up like Gaia Moore and scurry out into the street just to confuse whoever was watching her, baiting him into a full-blown wild-goose chase. They'd all pretty much done it just as a lark, but deep down Heather knew better than that. Nothing involving Gaia was ever just a lark. Some part of Heather had known that it was probably the bravest, most heroic thing she had ever done. And for a girl who was supposedly her sworn enemy, no less.

Heather still wasn't totally sure why she'd done it. Maybe it was just for Ed's sake, because he'd asked her to help, because she felt so guilty for being such a selfish bitch to him all these months. But she liked to believe that it was something nobler. She'd sworn to herself and to Ed that she was turning over a new leaf, becoming a far less selfish person from now on. And she'd been reveling in the fact that her new leaf was more than just another one of her empty self-help resolutions. This time she'd actually backed it up with some legitimate action. Helping Gaia was the first thing Heather had done in months that had made her feel truly unselfish. Truth be told, she'd been glowing with pride about it for the rest of last night.

But there was no point in celebrating her newfound altruism if her little maneuver hadn't in fact helped Gaia. And judging from the look on Ed's face, it seemed that might be the case. Much to Heather's amazement, she was genuinely worried as well.

"What happened?" she asked.

"What do you mean?" Ed muttered.

"*Last night,*" she pressed. "What happened last night?"

Ed turned back to Heather, offering her some fleeting eye contact, and then he began to unpack for class. "I have no idea," he said, void of any emotion.

"What do you mean. . . ?" She darted her eyes back toward the door and lowered her voice. "What do you *mean,* you have no idea? What happened with Gaia?"

"I have no idea," Ed repeated.

Silence again. Ed's sudden hostility felt like a sucker punch right to the face, and Heather wasn't sure how to react. She watched him fiddle with his bag, taking out a different pen and flipping blindly through his copy of *Heart of Darkness,* the book they were currently reading in MacGregor's class. Small tears streamed from his eyes again, even though his face revealed no feeling.

"You *are* crying," she confirmed. "Jesus, what's going on? You have to tell me."

"There's nothing going on," he insisted, wiping the tears from his cheeks again as if they weren't there. But clearly something was either very wrong or else Ed was just sickeningly in love with Gaia Moore. Most likely it was both.

Heather's usual resentment was still too dampened to really erupt. "Look," she said, checking the doorway of the classroom again, "I put my neck out for her, Ed. The least you can do is tell me what happened."

"I don't know what happened."

"What do you mean, you don't know? Where is she now?"

"I don't know!" Ed snapped, finally looking her in the eye and giving her a glimpse of just how much pain he'd been working so hard to mask. "I don't know where she is. I haven't heard from her since yesterday. I don't know. . . ."

Heather stared at him. She loved him more than ever for those few short seconds. And then she was unimaginably jealous of Gaia for the next few. Gaia didn't deserve to be loved this much. What had she done to deserve this kind of love? But then again. . . what had Heather done to deserve that kind of love? Nothing. Nothing at all.

"I'm sure she's all right," Heather heard herself say as she placed her hand tentatively on Ed's shoulder. "Don't worry, okay?"

"I'm fine," Ed replied automatically. He shifted his shoulder almost imperceptibly, moving it just far enough to avoid Heather's touch without being obvious. Heather felt a gaping hole open up in her stomach.

"I—I just. . . ," Ed stammered. "I can't. . . I gotta go," he finished, shoving his stuff back into his bag and picking up his crutches. "Tell MacGregor I got sick, okay?" He hobbled by Heather and headed for the door.

"Ed," she called to him as he opened the door. "Really. You know you don't have to worry about her."

"Yeah, thanks," he muttered, letting the door swing closed behind him.

"I'm sure Gaia will be fine," she said. But she was speaking to an empty classroom. "*I*, on the other hand. . ."

There was no need to finish her sentence. No one was listening.

"THEY CALLED IT PROJECT INTREPID,"
Oliver said, sifting through
the thick binder's pages.
"They knew a lot more
about genetics and molec-
ular biology than they were
letting on in 1983—"

Government Guinea Pig

"I don't want a history
lesson," Gaia stated. "Just tell me what this all means."

"This isn't just history," Oliver said. "This is *your*
history." He glanced at her to be sure she wanted to
hear more. She confirmed with her silence.

"They were certain a war with Russia was just
around the corner," he went on. "And they wanted to
arm the American soldiers with every possible advan-
tage. It didn't take a genius to pinpoint the greatest
disadvantage for any soldier: fear. A good soldier was a
brave soldier—a man who'd cross enemy lines and
sacrifice his life without an ounce of hesitation.
Without a second thought. Excuse me, I should have
said a man or a woman."

Gaia was both sickened and mesmerized. Every
word out of her uncle's mouth made her more ill and
somehow colder, as if she were being slowly dipped in
ice water. But she was dying to hear more.

"I'll get to the point," Oliver said quietly. He'd
obviously noticed the pain he was causing her. "The
point is, the government had been studying fear from

a biological standpoint for years, and by '83 they'd finally mastered the biochemical process. So much so that they were confident they could *reverse* it. So they engineered a serum—a serum that would, in effect, block the chemical reactions that cause fear. And it worked, Gaia. It worked on rats, and it worked on chimpanzees. It was time to test a human subject."

Oliver flipped back to the first photo he'd shown Gaia. The picture of her father and those men in white coats. And that small baby.

"Tom Moore had been selected to assist the scientists on Project Intrepid," he said, "and Tom Moore had just had a daughter. The perfect human subject. . ."

Gaia's hand latched onto the binder and slammed it closed. It was a reflex that surprised her almost as much as it seemed to surprise her uncle. "That's enough," she announced, backing away from the desk coldly. "This is all bull. You've put this whole thing together. My father wouldn't have done this, and even if he had, he wouldn't have lied about it."

Gaia wanted to believe her own words. She said them as if she believed them, as if she was sure of them. But the fact was, she didn't trust her father any more than she did her uncle at this point.

"Now, you listen to me," Oliver said, rising out of his chair and approaching her with determination. "You wanted the truth, so I'm giving it to you. These are the facts: your fearlessness is *not* genetic. That is a lie your father told you as a child. Your fearlessness is chemical, injected into you at birth before you could have any say in the matter. The truth is your father offered you up as a government guinea pig with no regard for your feelings or your safety. He stole your humanity before your life had even started. He turned his own baby daughter into an experiment."

Gaia was unable to talk back. Now was the time to lash out, to hurl a long list of expletives and accusations at her uncle. To defend her father's honor and recount his twelve years of perfect parenting before everything had gone so miserably wrong. But all she could muster was some halfhearted verbal resistance.

"That could be any baby in that picture," she said. "You could have doctored that picture with my father's face."

"I could have, but I didn't." He moved a step closer. "And you know I'm telling you the truth. I can see it in your eyes. You're starting to understand what he's done to you. All those years of training you for battle. All those years of programming your mind and your body . . . and then he leaves you to fend for yourself at age twelve? He's *testing* you, Gaia. They're still testing you, do you understand that? He's not interested in how his daughter is doing. They just want to see how their fearless *specimen* will react to 'adverse stimuli.' It's disgusting. It's dehumanizing."

Gaia wanted to hide from her uncle's diatribe and avoid his penetrating stare. She wanted to climb under the huge mahogany desk. Her perfect childhood memories were her only remaining solace. She'd turned to those glorified memories of her mother and father time and again whenever things got unbearably dark or too existential. The distant past was really the only thing in her life that had stayed intact. And now it seemed that, too, had been slated for immediate demolition. But it all made sense. Gaia couldn't deny that. Every word out of his mouth rang true. And here were the pictures to prove it.

"You could have had a normal life," Oliver stated coldly. "He stole that life away from you. And that's why I've brought you here. . . ." Finally his dark expression began to ease up. The veil of menace in his eyes peeled away. "To give it back."

Gaia stared blankly at her uncle. She could muster nothing other than puzzlement at this point. "What are you talking about?"

"I'm talking about an antidote," he replied. Suddenly his mouth spread into a wide grin. He smiled at her like a proud father holding out the largest of all her Christmas presents. "That's why you're here, Gaia. That's why I've been trying to steal you away from Tom all this time. I thought they'd have to administer it in Germany, but they've agreed to come here."

"Who?"

"The *doctors*," he said, trying to enlist her excitement. "I've had them examining the file for years, trying to develop a compound that would reverse the effects of the initial serum. And they've *done* it, Gaia." Oliver's grin was so generous and gleeful, it barely fit his face. "We can undo all the damage Tom has done. With this antidote you could start from scratch. You would feel fear. You would finally know what it feels like to be a member of the human race instead of a fugitive from it. . . ."

All his words began to melt together in her ears. He might still be talking, but a loud drone had taken over as Gaia watched him tempt her with his overflowing optimism. She was in suspended animation, free falling somewhere between reality and fiction, and she didn't know where to land. She'd just had her entire life chopped into jagged pieces, shoved in a blender, and re-fed to her in a few painfully surreal minutes. And now she had no idea what she should be thinking. Slowly her uncle's words began to cut through the haze again.

"But I'm not Tom," he said with an intense stare that demanded her attention. "Unlike him, I wouldn't dare to make this choice for you. I know I've brought you here by force, but that was only to bring you safely to this point."

He reached for Gaia's hand. She let him have it. She could hardly feel it right now, anyway.

"The choice is yours," he said. "If you don't want the cure, I'm not going to force it on you. You have to tell me what you want. Do you want a chance at a normal life? We can give it to you right now."

Gaia's mouth began to open, but she froze before she uttered a word. The answer to his question was so obvious, it was unnecessary even to speak it. But to reply so easily, without a hint of further consideration, was undoubtedly wrong. She could hardly process what was happening at this moment, but she knew at least that much.

Here she was again with one of those unbearable choices. It was the most bizarre catch-22 she'd ever encountered. Perhaps if she could feel fear—if she could just be terrified by his offer—then she could say no. For all she knew, "no" was probably the correct answer. But she couldn't know that unless she felt fear. And the only way she might feel fear. . . was to say yes.

Once again, being fearless made her decision-making process feel utterly detached. The facts as she saw them were these: If her uncle was lying, if he'd fabricated this entire story as a manipulation of some kind, it really didn't matter. He'd already captured her. She was trapped no matter what her answer was. But if he was telling the truth. . . if her father and the Agency really had done this to her, if they really had made her into what she was today. . . then this would be a legitimate chance to start again—to fill in everything that was missing. Her fearlessness had become more of a curse than anything else. She wanted nothing more than to scrap it. To scrap her entire life and start over with a new name and some version of a real life.

Any way she looked at it, there was nothing else to

lose and at least *something* possibly to gain. Logic had left her with only one answer.

"I'll do it," she said. She let her mind and her body go numb, relaxing into the possibility that she'd just voluntarily made the biggest mistake of her life.

A wave of celebratory relief passed over her uncle's face as he pulled her into his arms for a hug.

"I'm so glad," he murmured. "I'm so glad, Gaia. I'll go get Dr. Kessler."

Gaia was neither elated nor sad. Nor was she particularly confident about her decision. She simply felt at the end of her rope and tired of running. It was either time for a new beginning or it was time for the end. Gaia didn't much care which one at this point. She really felt nothing other than the distinct desire for her uncle to remove his arms from around her shoulders.

"WE STILL DON'T HAVE A LOCK, SIR."

The voice was barking through Tom Moore's cell phone, penetrating his eardrum with each harsh consonant. He felt his throat constrict.

"What do you mean, you don't

Maximum Force

have a lock?" he shot back. "I thought we had location confirmed."

Tom yanked his steering wheel to the right and screeched onto Seventh Avenue, heading downtown. He'd been leaning hard on every single government agency at his disposal—the CIA, the FBI, even the NYPD, pushing them incessantly for leads on his daughter's whereabouts. There had been nothing for hours, not since surveillance had lost her in the early morning when she'd jumped into a black limousine in front of Ed Fargo's building.

It was bad enough that he'd been forced to waste an entire night clearing up his mistaken identity with the Agency. The Agency had actually allowed Loki to escape and had taken Tom into custody. It had taken hours of code checking before they'd finally confirmed that Tom was in fact Enigma and not Loki. But by the time Tom had been released, Gaia was already gone.

The fruitless search had left Tom in a state of panic, but finally the last hour had produced a legitimate lead. They had a building confirmed on West Twenty-ninth Street. At least that's what they'd told him.

"Sir, yes, sir," the voice replied through the insufferable digital static. "The building is confirmed, but we can't secure visual contact. No chance from outside the location, and he's got the inside fortified with seven to ten armed guards, sir."

"Contain the guards and get your team in there!"

Tom ordered. A taxi cut right in front of him with no warning. Tom slammed on the brakes and nearly swerved off the street, trying to recover without a full-blown ten-car pileup in the middle of Times Square. He ignored a circus of blaring horns and street rage, staying focused on the one goal of making it to Twenty-ninth Street in as few minutes as possible.

"We don't have any time for protocol here," he shouted. "My daughter may be lying dead in that building, so you get your people through those guards and into that room, do you understand?"

"Sir, yes, sir, I understand, but casualties will be—"

"But *nothing*," Tom snapped. "You're trained for top priority, and this is top priority. If Loki gets what he needs from my daughter, then we've got a massive threat to national security on our hands, so this debate is *over*. I am authorizing maximum force. Send in your team. That's an order."

Tom snapped his phone closed and crushed his foot on the gas pedal, doubling the speed limit as he raced down Seventh.

"Come on," he groaned with simmering impatience. "Come on. . . ."

His eyes darted back and forth between the road ahead and the numbered street signs up above. Thirty-seventh Street. Thirty-sixth. Thirty-fifth, Thirty-fourth. . .

"Stay strong, Gaia," he mumbled to himself. "Hang on."

She'd just started an entirely new life here on the bloody, glass- **normal** covered rug of this tastefully eclectic torture chamber.

"MAY I SAY IT IS A PLEASURE TO finally meet you, Ms. Moore."

Dr. Kessler raised his hand out to Gaia. He was younger and more handsome than she'd expected. When her uncle had mentioned the Germans, Gaia had instantly pictured a group of white-haired gentlemen with thick mustaches in the vein of Einstein and Freud. But with his dark, brushed-back hair and square jaw, Dr. Kessler looked more like he'd stepped out of a European car ad.

"You may say whatever you want," Gaia replied blandly, shaking his hand. The situation was too overwhelming for her to do anything but fall back into her default sarcastic mode.

"Yes. . . well. . . ," he replied awkwardly. Maybe they didn't have sarcasm in Germany. Or maybe he found the situation as overwhelming as she did. "I'll need you to sit here in the chair so we can get started."

She sat down, locking eyes with her uncle. He stood a few feet behind the doctor, seemingly nervous.

"Don't worry, Gaia," he said. "Dr. Kessler is an absolute expert. You're in the finest hands imaginable."

"Your uncle is too kind," Dr. Kessler said, flashing a brief smile as he stretched on a pair of latex gloves. He tied a rubber strap around the lower end of Gaia's thick biceps and tapped a vein of her inner left arm. "Now lay your arm down here, please."

Gaia let her arm rest on the extended arm of the chair, the same chair into which she'd been strapped not so long ago. It was more than a little disturbing as she flashed back to her first few moments in this room. The moments when she thought her life was nearly over. In a way, she supposed, her life *would* be ending. Her life without fear, that is.

Quite suddenly Gaia jerked her arm from the doctor's grip. It had hit her unexpectedly, but a sudden blast of doubt was rushing through her body like a chill.

"What's the matter?" her uncle asked brusquely, almost as if he'd been holding his breath the entire time.

Gaia had been so busy trying to weed out her uncle's lies and searching for the truth that she really hadn't stopped to consider what she was about to do. She'd been so focused on the past that she hadn't stopped to think about her potential new future. She was about to embark on a new life. A normal life of some kind. But what exactly would that be? What would her life be if she weren't fearless?

How did it feel to kiss a boy when you were feeling fear?

"NOTHING'S THE MATTER," GAIA
said, relaxing her arm back into the
hands of Dr. Kessler. "Everything's
fine."

Seizure

The tension dropped from Oliver's
face as his smile resurfaced. "Good, good." He placed his
hand on Dr. Kessler's shoulder. "Let's continue, then."

Dr. Kessler smiled kindly at Gaia and then strapped
her wrist down on the arm of the chair.

"What are you doing?" Gaia asked.

"This is just to avoid any more sudden move-
ments," the doctor replied in a soothing tone. "We
wouldn't want you to get hurt." He gave her another
friendly-neighborhood-doctor grin.

"Let's just get this over with," she mumbled.

"Yes, of course," he agreed, seeming to do his best
to diffuse the uneasiness building in the room. "I'll
just need a blood sample before we get started." He
was working so quickly that Gaia had barely noticed
the needle. The next thing she knew, she felt a slight
prick and then watched as he filled two vials with her
blood. "This is just to be sure we administer the right
levels of the serum," he said.

"Good," Oliver chimed in. "I want to be sure we've
taken every precaution for her safety." He smiled at
Gaia. She didn't smile back.

She knew that her uncle was ostensibly doing this
all for her, but that wasn't how it felt. Oliver was taking

such pleasure every step of the way; it felt more like this entire process was for his benefit. Every feeling Gaia was unable to experience, her uncle seemed to be having for her. He was more enthusiastic, more nervous. . . maybe even scared. It was disconcerting. Annoying. It felt wrong.

The doctor scanned her blood under the microscope, then he picked up a syringe filled with a liquid that hovered somewhere between clear and yellow.

"Now, a couple of things you should know," the doctor said, tapping the needle as he approached her. Suddenly Gaia found his German accent vaguely disturbing. "All our tests have shown that the serum should take effect immediately, although we really can't be sure of that in this case. You are, after all, our first human subject."

There was that word again. *Subject.* Gaia despised it. Especially when it was used in reference to her.

"There will be some initial side effects," the doctor continued. "Possibly drowsiness, disorientation. You may develop a high fever. I'm sure your uncle will take care of you, though." He smiled and turned back to Oliver.

"Yes, of course," Oliver replied. "I'll be watching over her every minute of every day."

"Good," Dr. Kessler said, turning back to Gaia. "Then I suppose the only thing left to say is. . . hold still."

So this was it. Assuming this serum was for real,

this would be Gaia's last official moment of being unequivocally fearless. And she could think of no moment more appropriate than this one. Because this moment—just before an injection of God knew what, by a complete stranger, in front of a man who had been her worst enemy up until only twenty minutes ago—this moment should have been terrifying. It should have been avoided at all costs. Gaia knew this with every ounce of her reason and wit.

But the only thing she felt was deep curiosity. The serum could be anything on God's good earth— cleaning fluid, steroids, heroin. . . . For all she knew, this was a lethal injection of some kind and her uncle had simply wanted to stretch out the process of murder for his own demented reasons. This could be her last moment on earth, and she could be about to find out the nature of the afterlife, not that she believed there was one. But she wasn't the least bit frightened. There was something rather tragic about that fact. Being fearless truly was a curse. She'd be ridding herself of a curse. Wouldn't she?

Gaia's face went blank as she glued her eyes to the needle and watched it penetrate her vein. Within seconds she felt the blast.

It was an explosion of excruciating pain that ripped through her muscles in one instantaneous chain reaction—as if her internal organs had been doused with gasoline and Dr. Kessler had just lit a match and dropped it down her throat. Her muscles began to constrict one by one involuntarily, curling in on her like a grand mal seizure. Her body became so contorted from the relentless sting that she froze in the same catatonic pose as an electric chair victim.

"Is she having a seizure?"

She could hear her uncle's voice dripping with anxiety, and she could see his face blurred with fear as he grabbed the doctor's shoulders and shook him for quick answers. But she couldn't utter a word.

"I . . . I don't know," the doctor muttered. He clamped his hands on Gaia's face and stretched her eyes open, peering into her pupils. "We didn't anticipate this reaction."

"Well, for God's sake, do something!" Oliver barked, grabbing Gaia's arms for lack of any other gesture. "Gaia, are you in pain?"

Gaia couldn't muster an answer at this point, nor would she have dignified such an idiotic question with a response. She had to control the pain. She had to overcome it. She shifted all her focus to her fingers, trying to will the exquisite aching from each digit, pushing to uncurl the right hand so she could shove her uncle out of her face.

Dr. Kessler grabbed her left wrist. "Her pulse is racing," he said, moving his fingers to her neck for another reading. He looked into Gaia's eyes. "Ms. Moore?" He'd raised his voice and begun to overenunciate his words.

"Ms. Moore, can you hear me?" As if Gaia couldn't hear his booming Germanic voice. *I'm sitting right here. I'm just in agony.* "Ms. Moore, can you say something? Can you speak to us?"

"Gaia, can you talk?" Oliver pleaded. "I'm right here, sweetheart, can you speak to me?" Gaia clamped her hand on her uncle's wrist. And with his eyes this close. . .

Somehow, in this pain-induced near-dream state, with his face only inches away, she could finally see something behind those ice blue eyes. The thing she'd been looking for the entire time. Something sinister and fundamentally false.

Yes, she could speak now. She was sure of it. Slowly she forced the words out through her clenched teeth. "What did you do?" she uttered, searching her uncle's eyes accusingly. "What did you do to me?"

She could swear she saw a momentary lapse in his fatherly guise. For one subliminal tick she was almost sure she'd seen through to the cold and heartless void behind all his kindness and concern. But she'd never be able to prove it, and she wouldn't get her answer. Because all the attention in the room had shifted to the door and the sound that had just exploded in the other room. The sound of rapid automatic gunfire.

It erupted from the other side of the opaque glass door in a storm of ear-shattering mechanical clatter.

The sound of piercing shots suddenly reverberated from every wall.

Oliver didn't speak another word, nor did he bother to check the door. He turned with a catlike reflex, grabbed the two vials of Gaia's blood from the medical tray, and took two smooth steps to a door in the back of the room. Gaia hadn't noticed it before. It was an old-fashioned door, designed to blend in with the patterned wallpaper and the wood molding. He unlatched it and stepped through quickly. The doctor tried to also, but the door had already been slammed in his face and locked. Gaia could see the terror in the doctor's eyes as he turned back toward the sound of screaming injured men coming from just outside the room. He pounded on the hidden back door repeatedly, calling out Oliver's name. But there was no response.

Gaia willed her throbbing legs to step from the chair. But before she'd gotten her first foot down, the entire room shook from floor to ceiling. A blood-soaked body shattered the glass of the front door, driven by the force of spraying bullets. It landed on the Moroccan rug `like a two-hundred-pound rag doll`. Black bullet holes were exploding in long successive rows across the walls, destroying every delicately placed frame and *objet d'art*. Gaia dropped to the floor and threw her hands over the back of her head, feeling a sharp spike of glass puncture her cheek as she hit the ground.

She heard the doctor plead momentarily for his life. "Please, I'm not part of this. I'm only—" His pleas were cut short by five deafening shots, followed by a loud thud and crunch as something massive hit the floor only inches from Gaia's head. She turned up her face and realized she was staring directly into the motionless eyes of the doctor, who was now sprawled out on the ground next to her. She watched as his lifeless eyeballs filled slowly with blood. His neck was twisted in an inhuman position, and blood poured from a thick hole at its center.

And suddenly a very new and horrid sensation had taken over Gaia's body. It wasn't the wrenching pain induced by the injection; it was something else. Something Gaia had never felt before and thus could hardly describe. It was *like* pain, but it affected no specific part of her body. It felt like the dark and miserable flip side of being thrilled. This torturous hollow buzzing made her heart race and drenched her in cold sweat.

Gaia shut her eyes. She couldn't bear to look at the doctor's dark red eyes for another moment. She couldn't bear the gunfire and the blood and the primal screams of all these brutal and efficient murderers, whoever the hell they were. She was in pain, and she was. . . desperate. . . .

I'm scared.

That had to be what this was. Fear. Didn't that have to be what this was? This awful racy feeling. This overabundance of sweat. This desire to hide her eyes from death and destruction. When had Gaia ever wanted to shield herself from blood or mayhem or. . . anything? This had to be fear or some version of it. The injection, it seemed, wasn't a fraud. She was almost sure of it.

So now what? she dared herself. She'd just started an entirely new life here on the bloody glass-covered rug of this `tastefully eclectic torture chamber`. She wasn't about to let it end only two minutes in. This moment, in its own twisted way, was something Gaia had been looking forward to her whole life. A chance to overcome fear. A chance to be brave, just as she'd promised herself only minutes ago. *You want to be brave? Then get your head out of your hands and get off the floor.*

She didn't pause to think again. Nor did she pause to feel this dreadful alien sensation or the merciless ache in her muscles and joints. She simply raised herself to her feet and reacted.

The shiny black metal of a rifle was in her face. She grabbed it with both hands and shoved it back into the black-hooded face of her assailant, denting his nose with a high-pitched crack. He let out a howl and dropped to the ground, writhing in pain.

Two more hooded gunmen loomed directly behind him. They charged at her. Gaia ducked to the floor, tucking her body into itself and becoming a stumbling block for the attacker to her right. She ripped the machine gun from his hands as he toppled over her and then whipped the butt of the gun against his head before he'd even had the chance to reorient himself. The second man lunged for her, but she crammed the barrel of the rifle deep into his stomach.

"*Oomph*," he groaned. The gun fell from his hands, and he doubled over. Gaia didn't give him another moment to think or regain his balance. She zeroed in on his chin and snapped his head backward with a pinpoint front kick to the face. But there were already two more coming at her from either side.

She used all the momentum of one to flip him a hundred and eighty degrees and send him crashing into the other. It might have looked like the playful stunt of a professional wrestler, but the sound of the collision was more like the blunt, unholy thud of a traffic accident. She heard no cries of pain, as they had clearly gone unconscious on impact.

Gaia whipped around for the next attack, but when her body stopped spinning, her field of vision did not. The entire room began to tilt to the right, twirling around her `like a carousel on fast-forward`. And she couldn't make it stop. She could see more hooded soldiers in black, but they seemed to have gathered in a circle around her and begun to revolve, like a vindictive gang of taunting terrorists playing ring-around-the-rosy. She tried to narrow her focus, but it was impossible. Everything had turned into one big peripheral blur. Not only was the room spinning, but the lights had begun to dim.

No, not now, she pleaded with her body. *Not yet.*

But it wasn't something she could control. She might have the bravery to take on ten men, but she'd overestimated her physical limits. Adrenaline had masked her substantial weakness for a few moments, but now reality was kicking in. Her strength had been ravaged by that injection. Her postbattle blackout was announcing itself prematurely. The room grew dimmer in a matter of seconds until it had begun to match the black hoods that surrounded her.

So this is it, she thought with cold resignation. Sixty seconds. Sixty seconds of a `"normal" life` was all she'd be granted by those assholes, the fates. One minute of bravery and now she'd be gunned down defenselessly. She wouldn't even be conscious for her own death. How perfect. How totally appropriate.

Gaia dropped to her knees, holding on to the last vestiges of consciousness as she felt what seemed like a hundred hands grab at her arms and stretch them—almost from the sockets. And then it was over.

I wonder what fear feels like?
It's the question I've asked
myself every day for as long as I
can remember. Until now—now I
wonder if I *want* to know what
fear feels like.

I mean, normal people would
probably think I was the asshole
of the century right now. As far
as I can tell, people spend at
least three quarters of their day
wishing they *weren't* so scared.
Scared of whatever—scared of the
dark, scared of boys or girls,
scared of failing trigonometry,
scared of their boyfriend falling
for that bitch who's always flirting with him. Scared of their boss
or their father or poverty or
loneliness or death. Everybody's
scared, right? Except me.

But here's the thing: at least
they know how to live a life
filled with different fears. They
know what life *feels* like. You
tell me, if it's such a gift to
be fearless, then why the hell
does everyone but me always seem

to be smiling so goddamn much?

I think I know why. I think it's because they're taking all these little pleasures every day that I know nothing about. It's like they can't even feel like valid human beings unless they're overcoming some kind of fear. That's what it is. That's what their smiles are all about. They smile when they get an A because deep down, they were terrified they'd fail the test. They smile when they get a job because deep down, they were afraid they'd live out the rest of their life unemployed until someone found them in a Dumpster clinging to a bottle of Jack Daniels. They smile when they get a date because deep down, they were sure they were going to end up alone in some rocking chair, knitting sweaters for their sixteen cats. Hey, they even smile when someone says hello to them in the hallway. Because somewhere in their fearful heads, they were actually worried that this might be the day when all their friends

took a private meeting and decided
to hate them for the rest of the
year.

　You know, come to think of it, I
guess fear can be a pretty pathetic
monster. But still. There's no
denying it. Overcoming these little
daily fears is what gives people. . .
I don't know. . . joy. It's what
gives them a reason to live, I
guess. So where does that leave me?

　I think I know the answer to
that question, though. I think a
lot of what I'll do every day will
be the same thing. Only now it
won't just be to pass the time. It
won't just be a way to cope. Now
maybe it will actually bring me
some joy. Maybe I'll experience
some of that mysterious pleasure
that I've been standing here and
watching everyone else have.

　Because I won't be fearless
anymore. No, this time I'll feel
the fear. . . and I'll overcome
it. I'll finally know what it
feels like to be brave.

His grin
doubled in
size as he
turned up
to the
woman's
face and
gazed at her
adoringly.

red

velvet

lips

"HEATHER! WAIT UP!"

Heather shut her eyes and froze at the end of the hall. It was Megan. *Dammit.* And Heather was only two steps from the stairs. She'd been paying strict attention to all of their schedules—Carrie, Megan, Melanie, and Laura—to make sure that she didn't run into any of them for the rest of the day. She'd made it as far as sixth period, but somehow Megan had caught up to her in the third-floor hallway. Heather hung her head. Megan must have bagged her last class just to seek Heather out. Just to get the scoop. The scoop that Heather didn't have.

Heather turned around slowly, applying the most comfortable smile she could manage. But the smile didn't hold. Megan wasn't alone. All four of them had apparently bagged their last classes and formed a very giddy semicircle behind her.

"What's up?" Heather asked, feigning ignorance.

"Come on," Carrie said, bouncing slightly in place. "Did we, like, save Gaia's ass yesterday or what?"

"Yeah," Melanie chimed in. "How did our faux-blond full-force posse work out?"

"Um, excuse me," Carrie said. "Quick correction. We may have all worn blond *wigs,* but we are not *all* faux blonds."

Faithful Soldiers

"Yeah, right," Melanie replied. "Why don't you just give me the three hundred bucks you spend at Privé every month, and then you can be officially discharged from the faux-blond full-force posse?"

I have to get out of here, Heather thought, suddenly feeling sick to her stomach.

"Okay, quick lesson," Carrie shot back. "Highlights are not faux; they are called *enhancements*—"

"You guys!" Laura interrupted. "Later, maybe, you think? Can we stick to the matter at hand here?"

"Yes," Megan bubbled apologetically. She turned to Heather. "The matter at hand. Is Gaia okay? What happened last night?"

Heather surveyed the well-made-up, perfectly coifed, desperately excited faces of her dear friends, and her sickness morphed into the very feeling she'd been trying all day to avoid. The feeling she'd been putting off ever since her unfortunate encounter with Ed.

The terrible feeling of failure.

The fact was, even if their little antistalker plan had been Gaia's idea, Heather was still the one who'd gathered her "soldiers" for the "operation." She knew her friends all had their own reasons for agreeing to the big stunt, but in the end they'd really done it out of loyalty to Heather. And now she felt. . . well, kind of like a general who'd led her troops into battle and couldn't even tell them who'd won the war.

"Um—um. . . ," she stammered through her smile. "I'm. . . not sure."

"What do you mean?" Laura asked.

"Did you talk to Gaia?" Carrie asked.

"Did you talk to Ed?" Melanie tacked on, overlapping them both.

Heather felt her toes scrunching inside her shoes. Had she talked to Ed? The one she'd risked her life for? And the lives of her friends as well? The one she'd been trying so hard to prove herself to, to make a real sacrifice for? Yes. She'd talked to him. He just hadn't really talked to her. In fact, he'd pretty much flat out ignored her.

Being confronted by her friends had only served to magnify the awkward and uneasy sensation that had been growing inside Heather since the morning. She had behaved more nobly than she ever had in her whole life. . . and the only responses she'd gotten so far were angry words and a door basically slammed in her face. She had no idea what to think. Was Gaia in much deeper trouble than she thought? Or had she just moved on from New York without a word, in her own inimitable, existential loner fashion? Maybe that was it. Maybe Gaia had just had it with New York and VS *and* Ed. Maybe that's why Ed was so upset.

Or did it have something to do with Sam? Maybe Ed was just sulking because Gaia had run off and worked things out with Sam. If that was the case, then welcome to the club, Fargo. Welcome to the side of Gaia Moore you seem to have been missing for the past year.

Whoa, Heather. Watch yourself. You're slipping.

She had to get hold of her frustration. She wasn't going to let herself slide back into selfish pettiness based on nothing but a bunch of unanswered questions. And that was really all she had right now. That and an increasingly frustrating sense of wasted nobility. And four friends who deserved better.

"I talked to him, but. . ." Heather left the sentence hanging.

"But *what?*" Megan asked insistently.

Carrie stepped forward. "Heather, hello, what's going on?"

"Yeah," Laura agreed, frowning. "Why are you acting so *weird?* They're simple questions. Is Gaia all right? And did you talk to Ed or not?"

The troops were getting restless. Simple questions, maybe, but not such simple answers.

"Well, here's the deal," Heather began, trying to share some reassuring eye contact with each one of them. "I *did* talk to Ed, but I'm not sure we understood each other so well." That was one way of putting it. "So I think we'll need to have another little chat."

None of them looked very happy with the reply. And Heather couldn't blame them. Her reply was lame. Unfortunately, though, Ed was the only person who had the answers they deserved. Which meant that she'd have to go back to him. A repeat of the morning's conversation was not high up on Heather's list of self-esteem builders, but she supposed it would have to be done. She would have to march back up to Ed for some well-deserved clarity. If not for her own self-esteem, then at least to satisfy her faithful soldiers. Although. . . probably more for her own self-esteem. And maybe it didn't have to be today. . . .

Hmmm. This whole "unselfish" thing was much harder than it sounded.

"GAIA? CAN YOU HEAR ME?"

The voice was so familiar. A man's. Her father? Her uncle? She couldn't think. Thinking hurt. Everything hurt so bad. Every limb on her body was being pecked by invisible vultures. Or could she see the vultures, hovering over her face? Were her eyes even open yet?

Steel Coils

She was so hot. Maybe she was in the desert? Buried in the sand? No, mud. She felt like she'd been buried in hot mud. . . or a cake? That was it. Someone had dropped her into boiling batter, and now they were trying to bake her into a cake.

"Gaia, open your eyes," the voice said. "You're safe now. It's over."

Fine. Just please turn off the oven and stick a fork in me. Her eyes fluttered open, but the shapes came much too close—the talking vultures, like white oval apparitions. Heads that could float. Or faces? Faces were watching her. Gaia chose the face hovering over her to the left and tried to pencil in all the missing details. The chin came through first, covered in salt-and-pepper stubble. Then the weathered cheeks and finally the translucent blue eyes. The eyes. . . *My uncle's or my father's?*

"Gaia, can you hear me?" he asked again.

"The oven," she whispered. "Please. Turn off the goddamn oven."

"I think she's delirious," the other face said. It spoke with the most beautiful Russian accent Gaia had heard since she was a child.

Or was it the same accent she'd heard as a child? That wasn't possible. Unless Gaia was dead and this hot and muddy desert cake world was heaven. . .

"Gaia," the man said with an angelic smile, "it's your father. I'm here now. You're safe from Loki. Can you hear me, sweetheart? There's someone here who wants to meet you. . . ."

His grin doubled in size as he turned up to the woman's face and gazed at her adoringly. Gaia turned with him, trying desperately to make out the face, trying to see if the face matched the unforgettable voice—the soothing voice that Gaia had wanted to hear ten times a day for the last five years. But it couldn't be who she thought it was. Could it? Maybe they were all dead now. All three of them. Was that possible?

Gaia raced from feature to feature, filling in every detail of this golden white apparition's face. Her red velvet lips, her elegant sharp cheekbones and creamy skin. *Maybe she never died? Maybe that was just a bad dream. The last five years, just a bad dream.* Her brown eyes flecked with orange, the dark glossy hair. . . She had to touch her to be sure. She couldn't just trust her vision. Not while she was in this miserable state of being cooked alive.

She reached out for the ghost. But she couldn't be a ghost because she took Gaia's hand. If she was just an apparition, then how could she be so real to the touch? Real flesh, gripping tightly to Gaia's hand. Blood pumping through the fingers and giving the cheeks a healthy red flush. She *was*. She was alive.

Gaia's mother was alive.

She was flesh and blood, and she was holding Gaia's hand in bed, just as she'd always done when Gaia was sick.

"I knew you weren't dead," Gaia whispered. A rush of tears began to flow from her glassy eyes and pour down her sweltering face. "I knew it."

"No, Gaia," her mother said, flashing her smile. "You don't understand, darling." Her mother laid her hand on Gaia's face and then turned worriedly to her father. "Oh God, Tom, she is burning."

"I know," he agreed, matching her mother's worried expression and looking down at Gaia.

"I am," Gaia uttered. "I am burning. Can we turn off the oven, Mom? Please?"

"What is she talking about?" a troubled voice chimed in from behind her mother. The question had been asked in Russian, but the voice was so incredibly familiar. A young woman's voice, somehow even more familiar than her mother's.

"*English*," her mother said, turning behind her. "We speak English now."

"Does she even know where she is?" the girl asked in a thick Russian accent.

"That voice. . . ," Gaia moaned, staring up at the ceiling. "Why do I know that voice?" She raised her throbbing head as much as she could, trying to see the young woman's face in the shadows. "I can't see you. Let me see you."

The girl finally stepped out from the shadows, and when she appeared in the light, Gaia felt all the blood drain from her body. The long blond hair, the excessively muscular frame, the permanent frown of muted bitterness in the lips. Gaia had stared at this ugly face a million times. She'd been disappointed by it,

69

cursed it, ignored it, but it never went away. Of course the voice was familiar. It was familiar because it was her own.

Gaia was staring at herself. She watched as her mirror image placed a hand on her mother's shoulder and stared down at her with a particularly cold scowl—even by Gaia's standards.

"What's the matter?" Gaia begged of her mirror image. "Why are you so angry at me?"

"Don't you know?" she spat back bitterly, staring into Gaia's eyes. "We're *dying*, Gaia." The anger began to drop away as tears fell from her eyes as well. "Don't you see what you've done? You've killed us. Now our whole family is dead."

"Shut up!" Gaia screamed, writhing in pain as she tried to climb out of the bed. "I'm not dead. You don't know what you're talking about." Gaia turned to her mother and grabbed at her arms. "Tell her, Mom! Tell her I'm not dead!"

Gaia's mother backed away and looked helplessly to her father for answers.

"Gaia, stop it!" her father shouted. He clamped his hands on her shoulders and struggled to push her back down on the bed. "Sweetheart, relax—you're delirious."

She raised herself far enough out of bed to take a swipe at her mirror image, but the apparition backed away before Gaia could get a good punch in. "You shut your goddamn mouth!" Gaia howled. "I won't die if someone will just turn off this oven!"

Her father held tight to her shoulders and pressed her back down on the bed. He shook her gently, lightly slapping his hand against her boiling face. "Gaia, listen to me," he said. "Listen to me. Loki gave you something. We don't know what it is, but it's given you a very high fever and you're hallucinating, do you understand me? You need to calm down. You need to relax."

Stitches of memory floated faintly through Gaia's mind as her father shook her: her uncle's satisfied grin, the syringe filled with yellowish liquid shooting deep into her vein, a warning from Dr. Kessler. "Possibly drowsiness, disorientation," he'd said. "You may have a high fever. . . ."

Her body felt like Jell-O spiked with steel coils. Her father's grip had shaken everything into a blur. The light slaps to her face were far more painful than they should have been. But as the vibrations began to subside, her surroundings started to come more clearly into focus. The shaking had actually done her some good. She was breaking from her feverish delirium and slowly returning to reality.

Yes. She was lying in a bed soaked through with sweat, in a room she had never seen before.

She turned to her mother. But this woman wasn't her mother at all. There was actually only the slightest resemblance. This woman's nose was much shorter, much less defined, without the long, perfect elegance of her mother's. And the shape of her face was completely different. Turning her head slightly, Gaia then saw that the girl she had seen as herself had even less of a resemblance. With the exception of long blond hair and an age range similar to Gaia's, she and Gaia really had very little physically in common. *She doesn't look like me at all. No, she's graceful and beautiful. Whoever she is.*

"I think she's coming out of it," Gaia's father said. The older woman flashed Gaia a warm smile. But the beautiful girl continued to stare at her, cold and distrustful, from the end of the bed. She took a step back into the shadow of the room.

"You see, Gaia?" the woman said in her thick but refined Russian accent. "You were right. You are not dead."

"Who are you?" Gaia croaked. She wiped the thick film of sweat from around her mouth. "Where are we?" Her vision was still blurry, and sound was still popping in and out. Continuous reality checks were a necessity.

The woman turned to Gaia's father as if it wasn't her place to answer Gaia's questions. He laid his sizable hand over Gaia's forehead and smoothed the moist hairs back from her face.

"Well, this is an awkward time for introductions," he said with a smile, "but there's nothing we can do about that now. Gaia, this is Natasha. Natasha is going to take care of you for a while, just while I'm away." He turned to the end of the bed, referencing the graceful girl hidden in the shadows. "This is Tatiana, her daughter. She'll be living with you as well."

Gaia felt like she was in some hellish reworking of the *Wizard of Oz.* Everything seemed otherworldly and tentative, and she felt much more like a child than she should have. She'd only been truly awake for a moment or so, and she still had very little faith in her ability to separate reality from dreams. "What are you talking about?" she asked, drowning in confusion. "Where are we?"

"We're home," he said. "On East Seventy-second Street." He smiled at that Natasha woman again. "This is going to be your new home for a while. When you feel ready to stand up, you can take a look around. It's really a beautiful apartment, Gaia. Natasha and Tatiana helped me pick it out. As a matter of fact, they are actually very distant relations of your mother's, going back a few generations on your grandmother's side. So I'd like it if you'd think of them as family."

Was this all a hallucination as well? What the hell was he talking about? East Seventy-second Street? Natasha and who? Did he say something about family. . . ?

The room was officially spinning again, which only brought Gaia back to the last conscious moment she could remember. Her uncle's makeshift lab spinning

73

around her ceaselessly. Being torn apart by all those black-hooded soldiers.

"There were so many of them," she thought aloud, aware that she was tangled up in non sequiturs at this point. "They were clutching me so hard. They wanted to kill me. What happened?"

Gaia's father turned away for a moment, almost as if he were ashamed. When he looked back at Gaia, all the joy and ease had been stripped from his expression, leaving only feeble humiliation in the furrowed corners of his mouth. "I think I'll always be apologizing to you, Gaia," he said timidly. "And here I am doing it again. It took us so long to find you. I'm sorry," he confessed with a catch in his voice. "But you're safe now, and you are alive. Believe me, Gaia. You *are* alive."

"But why?" Gaia asked. "Why didn't they kill me? They were shooting everything in sight. Everyone."

"They weren't there to kill you," he said. "They were there to *save* you. And they did their job. You'll be safe as long as you stay here, I promise you that."

"I don't understand," Gaia muttered, feeling her exhaustion winning out. "I don't understand anything you're saying."

The edges were all disappearing again, the entire room turning into nothing but floating objects free of gravity or shape. Her father's face was fading away.

"We'll explain it all when you're feeling better," he said. "I promise. I just need to catch up with Loki while the trail is still hot. He's done enough damage as it is."

Gaia's eyes were closing on her, the heat enveloping her body once again. But one last burst of memory sent a surge of anger through her chest—up into her swollen face, forcing her eyes back open. She grabbed her father's wrist, digging her nails into his skin, speaking with what little strength she had left.

"Was I your experiment?"

She glared at him, confused and unforgiving. Her father stared back at her, raising a deeply puzzled eyebrow.

"Just tell me the truth," Gaia insisted. "I don't care anymore—I just want to know the truth."

"What is she talking about?" Natasha asked.

"I think she's still delirious," her father replied, looking deeper into Gaia's eyes. "Gaia, what *are* you talking about?"

"Just tell me," she uttered as her voice became faint.

That burst of raw coherent energy had been her last. It was an aberration, and once again Gaia found herself unsure of where she was and whether or not she was awake. A feverish sleep began to swallow her up again.

"Gaia?"

"Tell me. . . ," she muttered, mostly to herself at this point. Even if he'd answered, Gaia wouldn't have known it.

"TOM, JUST HEAR ME OUT—"

"George, *please*," Tom interrupted, rising from George's couch for another cup of coffee. "This is not a subject for debate."

Family Portraits

"But how well do you know the woman?"

Tom stepped into the kitchen and dumped another splash of black coffee into his mug, but that would be his last. He'd stopped at George's town house for one final briefing, but it had already become far less brief than he'd intended. It was foolish to leave Loki even an hour of leeway, let alone the half day Tom had already spent making arrangements. George couldn't have picked a worse moment to introduce antagonism into their friendship.

"I *told* you." Tom groaned. "Natasha's record is impeccable. She's one of the top ten agents in the Eastern sector. She's got more successful ops under her belt than seventy-five percent of the Agency. And she's part of Katia's *family*, George. I don't care how distantly they're related. Family in Russia means loyalty, and that makes me more secure than any statistic possibly could."

"But leaving Gaia with total strangers," George mumbled as he stepped into the kitchen.

"Natasha and her daughter are not strangers, George. They're family—"

"They're strangers to *her*, Tom," George interrupted. He locked eyes with Tom, placing himself in the way of the kitchen door. His plea for Tom's compassion felt more like a demand than a request.

Tom knew how much he was asking of Gaia, to make another adjustment to another foster situation, but he could see no way around it at this point. Not if he wanted to protect her. Not if putting Loki out of commission was going to get his full attention. He had to believe that Gaia's resilience would get her through the initial shock of boarding with a new family. Natasha and Tatiana would earn her trust. He might not know them that well, but he certainly knew them well enough to see their honesty and their kindness and their strength—all qualities Gaia was sure to appreciate.

But looking into George's eyes, so saturated with apprehension and caring, Tom realized just how far he'd regressed into tunnel vision the last few months. All this time George had been backing Tom up, taking the reins as Gaia's guardian at the drop of a hat, Tom really hadn't stopped to consider what Gaia had come to mean to George. He was a great friend and a deeply committed agent, but that couldn't account for all the enormous sacrifices he'd made. After all these years how could George not have developed a deep personal stake in Gaia's life? It was only human. Tom had never seen that as much as he did right now in George's eyes.

But he needed to be firm in his decisions. Wavering would only chip away at his confidence, leaving himself and Gaia that much more vulnerable to Loki's maneuvers. George's devotion was a blessing, to say the least, but this was no time to make Gaia's parenting any kind of democracy. It didn't take much for Tom to start second guessing himself on the choices he'd made with Gaia. And if he started down that road, he knew where he'd end up—huddled in a well of unfathomable self-doubt and self-hatred. He'd been there more than a few times, and he could ill afford to fall back into that well right now.

"I trust them, George," he said firmly. "That's all I have to say on the topic."

George didn't say a word. He simply marched back into the den. Tom followed, fighting his frustration.

He sat down on the couch directly opposite George so that they were face-to-face. George ignored Tom's eyes and focused instead on the photos by the window—framed Polaroids he'd taken of Gaia and Ella posing uncomfortably for instant family portraits. Gaia's face had never looked so dour, nor had Ella's smile ever looked so painfully forced. Why did George feel a need to frame and display such disposable gloom? Tom shook his head, pushing the thought from his mind.

"George, listen to me, all right? The situation is clear. All the old reasons for distancing myself from her have proved totally valid. You can't deny it. The closer I am to Gaia, the closer my brother becomes and the more she suffers. As long as he's still out there, my proximity to Gaia is just going to cause more damage."

"You're missing the point," George stated. "If you leave Gaia alone again with this Natasha woman, then you're hardly any better than *him*, Tom."

Tom could barely believe his ears. To hear his closest friend compare him to his sick brother was more than just a slap in the face, it was a full-scale emotional ambush. Even after searching George's eyes more closely, Tom still couldn't find an ounce of remorse or regret for having made such a blasphemous suggestion. "What the hell are you talking about?" he finally choked out.

"Tom, do you understand what's been happening here? Do you understand how cruel you've been to your daughter for the last five years?"

His words made Tom's heart shrivel. His feet clenched with tension. He was suddenly stuck in an icy tug-of-war between unbearable shame and irrepressible anger. He didn't know whether to agree and beg for George's forgiveness or rip his ignorant, shortsighted eyes out. But he was certainly leaning toward the latter.

"You know how tortured I've been, leaving her all this time," Tom uttered, feeling rage simmering in his chest and working its way up his neck. "You *know* it. Why would you want to rub that in my face, George? Why would you want to do that?"

"I just think Loki's got you rattled," George mumbled. "And it's affected your judgment."

"What?"

"Open your *eyes.*" George leaned in closer to him. "What do you really know about this Natasha and her daughter? I don't care how good her reputation is, and I don't care who her father's great-grandmother was. Is this really the best time to trust a stranger with your daughter? Is this the best time to leave Gaia alone in a totally alien environment? You're being callous and foolish, and Gaia's going to be the one paying for it."

"I don't have time to listen to this," Tom breathed. "You tell me what the hell else I'm supposed to do."

"You're supposed to leave her with someone you trust!" George shouted. "You're supposed to leave her with *me,* Tom."

Tom stared at him. "Is that what this is all about?" he squawked.

"I was practically the girl's father for a year," George shot back. "I did everything I could for her—"

"And so have I," Tom said. "You tell me, George, should I trust Natasha more or less than you trusted Ella?"

Once the statement was made, Tom knew he'd officially crossed an unforgivable line. He knew the kind of guilt George must have felt for loving and trusting Ella—who had not only turned out to be a spy for Loki, but had actually attempted to kill Gaia in cold blood. It was nothing less than cruel to rub that fact in his face. But Tom hadn't said it to be cruel. He'd only said it out of his own dire obsessive need to justify his choices. Especially after George had laid into them with such blunt disapproval. He needed George to recognize and confirm what an impossible task it was to protect Gaia and to make choices that would help her rather than harm her.

George's expression turned gravely serious. His anger no longer even seemed to be the issue. "What happened with Ella should be a lesson to you, Tom," he said. "You're making a terrible mistake—"

"I have to go," Tom interrupted, standing up. George had his own issues to deal with, whatever they might be, and he'd picked the absolute wrong moment to challenge Tom's fathering. It was out of line, and Tom had heard enough. He walked to the door.

"*I'm* her father, George. She only needs one."

The Phantom Zone

IT DIDN'T SEEM QUITE AS PATHETIC until he'd seen himself in the mirror. But Ed just happened to catch a glimpse of himself as he pressed down on the liquefy button. Now he was frozen in place, staring at his own sunken eyes as the loud whir of the blender echoed through the kitchen.

Milk shakes.

Gaia was gone, and Ed was churning out black-and-white milk shakes. It was time for a much needed sanity status check. Unfortunately, he looked like a zombie. There was no discernable expression on his face. The sacks under his eyes had turned a vicious shade of egg-plant, while the eyes themselves were a crackled road map of little pink high-ways and access roads—owing to that totally unexpected little bout with tears.

But maybe milk shakes weren't so bad. He'd tried every other way to cope, after all. He'd tried the business-as-usual approach by going to school. That had only left him with an embarrassing public display of idiocy in front of Heather. He'd tried sitting still in every chair in his house and lying in every bed. He'd tried listening to music, sleeping the rest of the day away, watching a movie, doubling his physical therapy regimen. . . but absolutely nothing worked. Gaia's face was still chiseled so deeply in his brain that it seemed to appear on any surface in his field of vision. Along with her neck. And her stupendous shoulders and her powerful legs and her gold-dusted hair. . . *Jesus, Fargo.*

Sanity status on a scale of one to ten? He figured about a negative three.

His only real goal at this point was to stop asking himself the same incessant questions again and again. *Where did she go, why did she go, is she injured, wounded, dead, why won't she call?* Maybe that's why he'd opted for the blender. At least the shrill sound of mechanical grinding could drown out all the questions in his head. Not just the questions, but the silence. The horrible sound of Gaia's *not* being there—

He turned off the blender. There was another sound, too. The most welcome sound in the world. The sound of the phone ringing.

A smile spread across his face. He'd known she would make contact somehow. He'd known she would find a way, no matter what the hell was happening to her. Ed smacked the blender out of the way, splattering its thick gray contents all over the kitchen table as he tipped his entire body toward the phone that was hanging from the wall. His crutches toppled to the floor with a clatter, but he hardly noticed. He nabbed the phone, leaving only one ice-cream-covered hand on the table to support his entire torso.

"Gaia!" he yelled. "I'm here, I'm here—"

"Oh my God," came a familiar voice, followed by an ugly, high-pitched giggle. "Could you sound any more desperate and hopeless? That's really not what women go for, Ed. Keep that up and you're going to send that girl running."

Ed's smile evaporated. It wasn't Gaia. It was his

asinine, moronic freak of a big sister, Victoria. He clamped his eyes shut and tried not to let this horrid unwanted surprise finish him off. At the very least his parents, his sister, and her horrible husband were all still off on their little upstate getaway. And that was pretty much the only thing Ed had going for him right now.

"What do you want?" he murmured through clenched teeth, looking down at the hand that was now soaked in half-blended ice cream.

"Jeez, what is *your* problem?" Victoria groaned. "We're just checking in to see if you're okay. Mom and Dad want to make sure you're not throwing any wild parties over there."

Oh, yes. That was certainly what he was doing. It was one big, wild, drug-crazed, promiscuous party after another at the Fargo residence. "I'm fine," he grunted.

"Well, you don't sound fine," she said. His sister's genius never failed to amaze him. "Is this about Gaia?"

Ed didn't utter a word. Of course it was about Gaia—she just *heard* him shout Gaia's name, hadn't she? All he could do was balance himself silently on the table and pray that she didn't pursue this line of questioning.

"It is, isn't it?" she pushed. "I don't get you two, Ed. Your whole 'best friends' thing. I mean, you broke up with Heather, right?"

Please stop talking. Please stop talking—

"It just doesn't make sense," she went on, stomping all over Ed's prayers. "You so obviously like her, Ed. I mean, does Gaia like you that way or not? Does she know you're probably going to make a full recovery?"

Ed shook his head slowly, once again questioning any natural law that could possibly place him and his sister in the same gene pool. He vowed to investigate the possibility of a clandestine adoption. Yes, as soon he was out of this abandoned depressive nightmare, he would prove that he and his sister weren't related. If only he could just switch his sister with Gaia. Put Gaia on the phone and send his sister out into the phantom zone—into the invisible limbo where Gaia was lurking.

"I really have to go," he uttered in a robotic monotone. "Tell Mom and Dad I'm fine. All right?"

"Come on, Ed—"

"I mean it," Ed snapped.

There was silence on the other end of the line as Ed's hand began to slip ever so slowly along the melted ice cream. He was forced to hold himself up with his elbows, which only crammed the phone farther into his face.

"Whatever, Ed," Victoria finally mumbled. "I was just trying to help you out. Give you the woman's perspective here. You obviously like her—I can tell by the way you answered the phone. But you're not going to get anywhere waiting around, believe me. You should just tell her, Ed. Just tell her and I bet she'll—"

Ed dropped the phone on the hook, grabbed one of his crutches, and hoisted himself back upright. *Ahhh.* Sweet silence. He had no choice but to hang up on his sister. He had to keep those phone lines open in case Gaia called.

Right. In case she called. That was a good one. What Victoria didn't understand was that Ed *had* told Gaia everything. And this was what he had to show for it. One spilled milk shake and another stretch of unbearable silence.

She also
realized
that there
was at
least **another**
one
merciful **foster**
aspect of
home
this life:
you only die
once.

THE ROOM HAD TAKEN ON THE PALE

The Same Face

lifeless gray of the city just after sunset. Loki hardly noticed that he was sitting in near darkness. He'd become so engrossed in the results of Gaia's blood tests that he was still using the dim natural light from the massive windows to read. The report consisted mostly of undecipherable pages of letters and numbers—the various compounds that made up Gaia's blood and tissue. He should have just asked the remaining doctors for a report in plain English. He was an expert in many things, but biochemistry didn't happen to be one of them, and it was becoming quite frustrating to read. Though not half as frustrating as Josh Kendall's ignorance.

"I don't understand it," Josh grumbled, slumped on one of the two black leather couches that made up most of the vast room's furnishings. His voice was laden with `testosterone and postadolescent impatience.` "Why aren't we doing something? They took out seven of our guys. They took Gaia. We should retaliate. We should strike back. What are we waiting for?"

"Calm yourself." Loki sighed from the corner of his mouth, keeping his eyes glued to the test results. "We need to take our time now. Rushing hasn't served us in the least. Rushing only leads to chaos. QR3 was a perfect example."

Josh went silent. After a tense pause he shot up from the couch and stomped across the long empty floor to the industrial-size refrigerator in the kitchen, then pulled out a bottle of imported beer with a loud clank and slammed the door shut. "Are you calling that an *accident*?" Josh asked sharply, flipping the top off the beer and taking a long gulp.

"What would you call it?" Loki asked, finally lifting his eyes from the pages.

"I'd call it murder," Josh replied, staring back accusingly. "You shot him right in the head. I don't understand what he did that was so bad, you had to shoot him in the head."

"He was incriminating me in front of Gaia," Loki argued, sitting comfortably still in his seat. "He was fingering me for Moon's death. You know I can't have that. Everything would have gone smoothly at the loft if QR3 had just kept his mouth shut. He should have taken his beating from Gaia and stayed quiet. That's what he was trained to do. That's what they were all trained to do."

"Well, there were plenty of other ways to shut him up," Josh challenged.

Loki studied Josh's mournful eyes from a distance. This empathetic reaction was surprising. It was worthy of some further investigation—later, when Loki had the time. He placed the test results on the glass table next to the couch and approached Josh curiously. The the sound of the heels of his shoes echoed loudly off the bare walls, which still smelled of fresh paint. "Does it upset you that I shot him?" he asked, examining Josh's face as if he'd sculpted it himself. "Does it feel like you've lost a brother?"

"No," Josh scoffed, shooing away the accusation. He dodged Loki and headed back toward the couch. "What, just because he has the same face as me? He's not my brother. It's not like we had the same mother or something. He didn't even have a mother." Josh turned away and took another long, uncomfortable swig of beer. "There just aren't many of us left, that's all—I mean, *them*. There aren't that many of them left."

"I know that," Loki said. "That's exactly why I'm changing the plan."

Josh gave Loki a puzzled stare. "What are you talking about? Since when are you changing the plan?"

"You don't need to worry about that," Loki said, walking back toward the couch. He switched on the small brass lamp on the side table. By this point the spacious loft was bathed almost entirely in darkness.

"Well, what are my new directives?" Josh demanded. He leaned his head over awkwardly, trying to win Loki's attention away from his work.

"Don't worry," Loki mumbled with a dry half smile. He didn't honor Josh's request for eye contact. "I think you'll be quite pleased with them."

"Well, what *are* they?" he pushed.

Loki slapped the tests back down on the table.

Perhaps it was QR3's untimely death that was making Josh so invasive and pushy. Whatever it was, Loki needed to cut it short before it caused any further disruption. He'd obviously have to give Josh something to appease him if he wanted him to stay quiet. It was not unlike dealing with an infant. "All you need to do for now is wait for your instructions," he explained, speaking as deliberately as possible. "I'm still ironing out the finer points. Once that deal is settled, our new agent will have full and unlimited access to Gaia and Tom. And when the time is right—only when the time is right—that agent will permanently remove Tom from the scenario. That will no longer be a concern of yours."

"But what about Gaia? What about all the plans you've made with the doctors?"

"I've already told you," Loki huffed. "The plans have *changed*. We have Gaia's genetic material—that's all we need from her." He raised the blood tests and waved them in Josh's face for clarity. "Now we just have to find out how Dr. Kessler's serum affected her."

"Why?"

Loki took a long, deep breath, realizing the extent of explanation that was required. He leaned forward from the couch to be sure Josh was paying close attention because his patience was wearing extremely thin. "The serum is basically. . . Are you familiar with the drugs in the antipsychotic category—Thorazine, Haldol, Risperdal?"

Josh's expression remained blank. Loki shook his

head and swallowed hard with frustration. "They're *medications*. They're administered to mental patients who suffer from schizophrenia and similar disorders. They help to reduce their frightening hallucinations and control their paranoia. To put it simply, this serum has the *opposite* effect of those drugs. Dr. Kessler's serum actually *induces* frightening hallucinations and paranoia. It's the ultimate test of her fearlessness. Do you see now?"

"I think so," Josh offered unconvincingly.

"Think harder," Loki ordered. "Gaia will be experiencing the menacing hallucinations and paranoid delusions of the average schizophrenic. If she can remain fearless under those extreme psychological circumstances, then we will know for sure that her fearlessness stems purely from her genetic code. We'll know that it is completely impervious to any external or psychological stimuli. We'll have the proof we need to continue on."

Josh sat in silence for a moment, and then he eased back in the couch, trying, quite arduously from the looks of him, to process all the information. His eyes rolled down toward the floor as he slowly formed his conclusions. Finally he brought his head upright and looked into Loki's eyes with a surprising degree of intelligence. "So basically. . . we're just trying to scare her."

"No," Loki said calmly as he leaned himself back on the couch. "We're trying to terrify her."

Repulsively Feminine

of horrid nightmares that she couldn't even remember, and she was thankful for that. Whatever they had been, they'd left her entire body shaking uncontrollably. Not only that, but she was also drenched in a pool of sweat so thick, it almost felt like she was in a shallow salty pond and she was the pond scum that had floated to the surface. But that simply didn't matter anymore. Because the moment Gaia had opened her eyes. . . she was there.

Gaia tried to stretch her swollen eyes wider to adjust to the beautiful bright light and witness all three elements in perfect harmony. Her mother's glowing smile was in delightfully close proximity. Her silky voice glided through an unforgettable Russian tune. And a spoonful of delectable cold borscht was being pressed to Gaia's lips and poured down her burning throat as she lay in bed. There was no sense to it, but Gaia didn't care. Her body ached too much to care. The fates had obviously taken a meeting, considered the amount of undue torture Gaia had been exposed to over the last few years, and decided to give her a gift. One of the only gifts she truly wanted. Her mother had been returned to her.

". . . So beautiful," Gaia breathed, reaching out her

numb fingers from the bed to caress her mother's cheek. "You *are*, Mom," she uttered. "So much more beautiful than me."

"Oh, *Gaia*." Her mother laughed with a dismissive smile as she always did when Gaia suggested it. She shook her head with bemused disapproval, speaking to Gaia with her elegant Russian accent. "Will you look in a mirror, for goodness' sake? Someday. . . someday you will look in the mirror and you will see what is real. Instead of all this foolishness in your head, no?"

"My head," Gaia croaked. "My head hurts so much."

"Mine too," her mother said, flipping her long, honey brown hair off her face. "The head hurts very much. You see? Like mother, like daughter."

"Your head hurts, too?"

"Yes." Her mother placed the spoon down in the bowl. She raised a finger to her forehead, rubbing her left temple. "It hurts," she complained. When she pulled her hand away, there was suddenly a dark red splotch on her skin where her finger had just been.

She picked the spoon up again, lifting another spoonful of borscht to Gaia's lips, but Gaia couldn't take her eyes off the dark red stain on the side of her mother's head. It grew darker by the second. Darker and darker. And then slowly the ugly, crimson splotch of skin began to bubble and crack, at first like a scab, but then like nothing Gaia had ever seen. Melting and deteriorating of its own free will until a dark red fissure bubbled to the surface. The fissure crackled across the wound until it split open, and small drops of dark blood began to trickle from the gash and roll down the side of her mother's cheek.

"Mom. . . ?" Gaia asked weakly. "What's happening?"

"It hurts me so much, Gaia," her mother repeated. "So much. . ."

"Mom, you're bleeding. . . ."

Her mother's head began to quiver. She let out a painful moan as her entire face trembled in agony. She clamped her hand against the bleeding wound, dropping the spoon into the bowl with a loud clank and splattering dark red borscht all over Gaia's white blanket.

"Mom?" Gaia had no breath left to support her voice. "What's wrong with you?"

"I'm bleeding, Gaia," her mother said. "You need to help me. It hurts so much."

Gaia pushed herself up from the bed and grabbed her mother's shoulders. "Just tell me what I can do," she pleaded. "Just tell me what I can do."

"Don't let me die again, Gaia." Her mother pushed both of her hands against her head and gasped for every breath. "Don't let him kill me again. *Please.*"

That awful hollow buzzing returned to Gaia's chest. The horrid sensation she'd felt when those men stormed her uncle's lab. But Gaia had no time to reflect on it. No time for any selfish internal debate as to whether or not she was again experiencing fear. She had to take action.

"God, I don't know what to *do*," Gaia shouted. "Let me see it." She grabbed at her mother's hands and tried to pull them away from her head, but her mother wouldn't allow it. "Mom, please! I'm trying to help you!" Gaia tugged and tugged at her mother's wrists.

"Gaia, don't!" her mother shouted. "Please don't!" Gaia used every ounce of her strength and ripped her mother's hands away from her head. And that's when the piercing crack of a gunshot echoed through the room. Her mother's head snapped to the right from the force of the bullet, exposing the smoking black hole that had erupted in her left temple. Gaia screamed as she held her mother's shoulders and watched her lifeless head fall forward over her chest. A steady flow of blood poured down from her head and soaked her white floral blouse.

But still her mother wasn't dead. Her hands sprang up and grabbed Gaia's arms as she lifted her wounded head to Gaia and shouted her name. She screamed the name again and again right to her face, shaking Gaia relentlessly. "Gaia! Gaia, look at me! Look at me!"

The more her mother shook her, the more her face began to change. Suddenly the wound disappeared from her mother's head. And then, piece by piece, her mother's face began to morph into the face of another woman. *I know this woman,* Gaia told herself as the stranger shook her aching body back and forth. *I know her name. . . . Natasha. Her name is Natasha.*

"Look at me, Gaia!" Natasha shouted. *"Look at me."*

And then she was back. Back somehow to reality.

Everything had become incredibly quiet. Gaia stared into Natasha's eyes and then rolled her own tired eyes around this strange room. She had no idea where she had just been. She couldn't have been asleep because she knew what it felt like to wake from a dream. But she hadn't exactly been awake, either.

The most inexplicable combination of sorrow and relief passed through her heart, which was now racing. Gaia would never see her mother again. She knew that. But she also realized that there was at least one merciful aspect of this life: you only die once. At least Gaia knew that she'd never have to watch her mother die again. In Gaia's dismal existence, that fact actually passed for relief.

She looked back into Natasha's eyes, squinting from the bright light by the bed. "Let me go," she breathed. "I'm all right—just let me go."

Natasha obeyed her request, freeing Gaia's arms from her firm grip. She helped to guide Gaia's head back to the cold, wet pillow. "We should change these sheets. They're soaked. When you feel strong enough to get up."

Gaia pulled her heavy head up on the pillow so she

could see the room better. Her sheets were now covered in dark red stains, as was Natasha's floral blouse. "What is it?" she asked.

"Borscht," Natasha said.

Poison, Gaia thought. *This woman was trying to feed me poison.*

Natasha leaned down to pick up the flipped-over bowl and spoon from the floor. She looked at Gaia uncomfortably. "You needed to eat, so I thought. . . I am very sorry if you thought I was your—"

"I didn't think anything," Gaia interrupted coldly. She didn't need to discuss a single element of her life or her past with this woman.

"It's all right, Gaia," Natasha said. "You have a very high fever. Yesterday, too, you thought I was—"

"Were you singing something?" Gaia cut her off. "Something in Russian?"

"Just a little song," Natasha replied.

"How do you know that song?" Gaia pushed.

"It's just a song," Natasha replied defensively. "All my family has been singing that song for generations."

Gaia didn't respond. The blurry film had finally cleared from her eyes, and she focused closer on Natasha's warm, glowing smile. There was something about it. Something that wasn't right.

Gaia let her eyes pan across the room. It was like surveying some kind of alien landscape. Everything about it was so mannered and pristine, so repulsively feminine. It had been painted some sort of textured cream color, with all the moldings and trim painted white. There was another bed on the opposite side of the room. Both bedspreads were white with a pale cream-colored floral print, although Gaia's was now covered in bloodred stains.

But there was an aspect to the room that Gaia had skimmed right over. She slowly turned her head back toward the dark corner on the opposite wall and confirmed it. There was a girl standing in the shadows. Gaia had seen this girl before, too. But she couldn't remember her name. Perhaps she'd missed her the first time because she always seemed to be hidden in darkness. Or perhaps, in this case, it was because of her outfit—white tailored shirt and cream-colored skirt. She was perfectly camouflaged against the wall. At least now Gaia knew who had decorated the room.

Everything about the girl was swanlike—as if invisible strings were holding up her head, her long, graceful neck, and all her limbs. Her blond hair was tied up tightly behind her head, so tightly that it almost seemed like her whole face had been pulled taut and tied behind her head. She remained stealthily still in the corner and stared, emotionless, at Gaia. No, she wasn't just staring. She was doing something with her hands. . . .

She was writing. She was jotting something down in a small black notebook. Gaia looked up at her invasive eyes. The girl wasn't just staring. She was *examining*. She was taking notes.

"What are you doing?" Gaia asked sharply from the bed. The girl slapped her book closed and hid it behind her back. She didn't say a word. She only looked at Natasha.

"It's all right, Tatiana," Natasha said to the girl. "Gaia is still very sick."

"Where's my father?" Gaia demanded, dissecting Natasha's wide smile suspiciously.

"He is gone," Natasha said.

"Well, when will he be back?" Gaia's eyes darted toward the girl in the corner. *Tatiana.* "I want to talk to him."

"No, no," Natasha said, placing her hand over Gaia's. Gaia quickly tugged her hand away. Natasha's smile curved down into an expression somewhere between sympathy and pity. "Oh, I am afraid your fever was too high, perhaps, when your father spoke to you."

"What are you talking about?" Gaia searched desperately through her memory banks. She'd had no sense of time since her uncle had pricked her with that sedative in the back of his limousine. How long ago was that? It could have been hours or days. She was reasonably sure she remembered her father speaking to her. Why else would she be asking for him at this moment? How else would she have known this woman's name was Natasha? But as for the details. . . Gaia was extremely weak on the details.

"Gaia, your father will not be coming back to this house for a while." Natasha leaned in closer. "We're all going to live here together now. You and Tatiana and me. Tom has helped me to get a job interpreting at the United Nations, so I will be able to take care of you both. This will be our home now. Until your father returns."

Gaia stared numbly into Natasha's eyes, watching the sadistic pleasure she was clearly taking in this turn of events. And Gaia found herself paralyzed. Not by the sweltering heat that had engulfed her entire body or the horrific reenactment of her mother's death. She'd just been overcome by sheer disbelief. Stricken by a level of disgust as yet unknown. It couldn't be that her father actually thought Gaia would accept such a fate. It couldn't be that he would be so foolish and ignorant and cruel as to believe that he could actually *drop* Gaia in another foster home with another set of total strangers. Strangers who, once again, clearly couldn't be trusted.

It was as if her father's sole purpose in life was to work as diligently as possible to prove himself an evil, heartless son of a bitch. Even if Gaia was nothing other than his fearless guinea pig—his *Project Intrepid*—even if he'd known when he left Gaia in George and Ella Niven's care that Ella would try to kill her, this offense was still by far his worst. Because this time her father knew exactly what he was doing by leaving Gaia. He knew the dangers. He knew what it would do to her heart and soul. And he did it, anyway.

And then her uncle's voice blew through her mind. Something her uncle had said about her father that suddenly made such undeniable sense. *He's testing you,* he'd said. *They're all testing you.*

Gaia slowly looked over at Tatiana, moving her eyes down toward her lower back, where her crisscrossed hands clung to her little book of observations. Then she looked back at Natasha. She fixed her eyes on Natasha's "kind" face, burrowing through her motherly facade to what was clearly a cold, calculating mind. "You know I can see right through you?" she said, struggling with all she had to tug her covers off. At least she was still dressed. That would make what she was about to do much easier.

"What are you talking about?" Natasha asked. "Please, you should keep the covers on."

Gaia forced all of her muscles to work, stepping out of the bed in spite of the overwhelming dizziness. She pushed her matted wet hair out of her face.

"Please, I do not think you should be standing yet."

"You can't keep me here," Gaia warned, backing toward the doorway as she shot bullets at them with her eyes. "You people are sick. Truly sick."

"Gaia, what are you talking about?"

"You tell him that I'm through taking his *tests.* Tell him I failed this one because I ran. A fearless person wouldn't run, right? Well, then I must be terrified because there's no way in hell I'm staying here."

"Gaia." Natasha rose from her chair and stepped toward her. "I think your fever has—"

"Don't take another step," Gaia warned, "or I swear to God, I'll break your neck. I'm sure you know I can do it. Just tell him. . . ." The mere act of standing had left Gaia weak and short of breath. But her anger was providing all the power she needed. "Tell him to stay the hell out of what's left of my life."

Gaia turned around and willed her legs to run. Natasha began to chase after her, but even in this state Gaia was too quick for her. She jogged through the alien rooms of the apartment, slamming each door behind her until she'd found the front door. She burst through and bolted down the building hallway, nearly falling down the entire first flight of stairs.

For a moment the stairs appeared to be rolling up toward her like a `high-speed cement escalator`. Gaia grabbed onto the railing and shut her eyes, struggling to regain her balance. When she opened her eyes again, the stairs had thankfully stopped moving. But Gaia wasn't so sure that *she* wanted to move. If the silent stillness of a stairwell was daunting, she couldn't imagine what the outside world would be like. One simple thought spurred her legs to take on the stairs. One simple wish would keep her moving.

Be home, Ed. Just please be home.

My father always told me I was beautiful.

"You're the most beautiful thing I've ever seen." He would say it at least twice a day, usually when I was in the midst of some extremely banal unbeautiful task—like unclogging the toilet or cleaning out the gerbil cage.

But even in fourth grade I was well aware of why he did it. God knows it wasn't because I was actually beautiful. I mean, at the age of nine, I swear the top half of my face had decided to grow to full size while the bottom half was still stuck in negotiations. No, he did it as what I would call "a noble act of compensation." That is to say, he did it so that I wouldn't feel ugly next to my mother, who was in fact, empirically speaking, the most beautiful thing my father or I had ever seen.

I know most nine-year-olds probably thought their mothers

were the most beautiful woman
they'd ever seen, but I was also
a lot smarter than the average
nine-year-old, and in my case,
the opinion was based solely on
fact.

Plus I also had a very
sophisticated understanding of
which elements combined to form
that superior beauty. While a
lot of kids were probably under
the impression that their mothers' beauty stemmed only from
the classic "unfettered smile,"
I knew that in my mother's case,
it was actually a precise combination of three things:

1. The unfettered smile
2. The scent that her cooking
   created throughout the house
   (particularly her borscht and
   her beef stroganoff)
3. The sound of her voice when
   she sang a Russian folk song

When these three elements were
in harmony, my mother took on
this otherworldly radiance that

was so powerful, it was nearly
blinding.

And now, somehow, due to some
sort of glorious mix-up in the
time-space continuum, that blinding radiance is shining in my
eyes again.

His eyes and
mouth were
contorted with a
look of
unfathomable
pain, like **home**
a living Rodin
sculpture—
an agonized,
tortured soul.

"TESTS? WHAT TESTS? WHAT ON

earth is she talking about?"

Tom felt a painful twinge in his stomach. He couldn't begin to understand the meaning of Gaia's statements, but it really wouldn't have mattered what she had said. Natasha's description of his daughter's bitter rage hurt enough.

Accidental Compliment

"I have no idea," Natasha replied, tightening her coat as the wind kicked up. "I don't know that she was in her right mind, Tom."

They were standing on a deserted steel platform under the Brooklyn Bridge, right by the South Street Seaport. The night wind had turned rather strong coming off the river, and the water was just rough enough to send some faint ripples onto the shore. Just below the steel platform was a thirty-foot span of garbage-laden rocks and sand. It was just about the only remaining evidence that this city had once been an actual island with actual beaches.

Tom kicked the metal rail with frustration. He knew how childish it must have seemed to Natasha, but it couldn't be helped. It *was* the act of a child. An involuntary response to his complete powerlessness.

"What did he do to her?" he murmured, staring out at the lights of Brooklyn. "I need to know what he did to her."

"We'll find out, Tom," Natasha said. "Don't worry." She placed her delicate hand on his shoulder and gave it a firm squeeze. Tom stiffened at her touch. He turned his head slightly to where her hand touched his shoulder. Natasha pulled her hand away, flashing an uncomfortable reassuring smile before she thrust her hand back in her coat pocket and turned out to the water. Tom felt a pang of guilt for having stiffened up, although he wasn't quite sure why. He moved quickly to the next moment.

"I *hate* not being with her," he murmured. "I know it's for her own protection, but it feels like I'm just leaving her hanging out there. I can't stand it."

"I'll take care of her," Natasha assured him. "You've made the right decision, Tom. She's in good hands with me, I promise you. So she needed to run off tonight. That's okay. Let her collect herself. We've got people keeping an eye on her at all times."

Tom nodded, although nothing could give him much solace right now.

"You need to understand something, Tom. . . ."

Tom kept his gaze locked across the water. The same question was still running through his head. *What did he do to her? I need to know what he's done.*

"Tom. . . ?" Natasha used the tip of her index finger to turn Tom's head to hers and establish eye contact. Then she quickly let go. Tom looked into her large brown eyes and gave her his full attention.

"No matter what she is going through," she said, "Gaia is still just a teenager, like any teenager. Like my daughter. Her anger is not only because of Loki. She is angry at having to move again. . . at having no real home." The wind was snapping Natasha's long, honey-colored hair all over her face. Tom felt compelled to reach over and sweep it behind her ear. Simply as an act of public service. But he kept his arm glued to his side. Thankfully she finally gathered it in her own hands and tucked it into the back of her coat. Her eyes dug deeper into Tom's. "She only wants what you want, Tom," she said. "A normal life. She wants her father. And she wants her mother very badly."

Tom lowered his eyes. He could feel the veins in his neck bulging as he strained to harden his heart. The simplicity of Natasha's statement had hit him with enough guilt to crush him against those jagged black rocks. Of course Gaia wanted her mother. Tom wanted her, too. But he had lost her. Thanks to one brief moment of ineptitude, he'd lost her for them both.

"You know. . . ," Natasha began cautiously, "she has mistaken me for Katia twice now." Tom raised his head again, locking eyes with her. "Our families are separated by many generations. Do I really look so much like her?"

"No, not really," Tom said dismissively. He had a flash of worry that his answer might have somehow come out offensive, so he quickly amended it. "I mean, you're both beautiful in different ways. . . ." Tom froze at the end of his statement. That was not at all how he had meant to say it. "I mean, I didn't mean to say that you were. . . Not that you're *not*. . ." Each addendum to his sentence made him more uncomfortable than the last until he'd finally talked himself into a painfully awkward silence.

Natasha smiled. "It's okay," she said. "Thank you for the accidental compliment."

Tom nodded and turned back toward the water, trying to find a professional way out of this deeply unprofessional moment. But Natasha did it for him.

"I should check in on Gaia. Make sure she is all right."

"Yes," Tom replied quickly. Natasha had brought them back around to the real matter at hand. "You'll let me know immediately. . . ."

"Of course," she said. "Don't worry, Tom. She's had a little time alone. I'm sure she must have calmed down by now."

Long Walk to Purgatory

FITS AND STARTS. THE ENTIRE CITY was coming through in fits and starts. Bells were too loud, lights were too bright. Sirens were making Gaia's ears bleed. Why was everyone screaming?

Spitting vicious curses at her for bumping into them? She wasn't even coming near them. No. . . that wasn't true. She was bumping into everything. Walls, mailboxes, fire hydrants, bitter old men, and mischievous children. Street after street, it was all the same. The sights, the smells, the sounds. Enough light to make her blind, enough garlic to make her retch, and this collective cloud of anger, firing random bolts of lightning into every malevolent stranger on every corner.

She had no idea how long she'd been walking or how close she was to Ed's. She only knew that her clothes were drenched with sweat and that people had gotten progressively uglier with every block. The image of Ed's kind and beautiful face was like a distorted phantom carrot, dangling just ahead to keep her moving forward. But no matter how hard she dragged her aching legs and no matter how far she went, she still didn't feel like she was moving any closer to beauty of any kind. It was quite the opposite. It seemed as if, without remembering why she had done so, Gaia had decided to take a nice long walk to purgatory. But she'd gotten there hours ago. She'd just been walking in circles ever since.

Burning up and walking in circles. She was past purgatory. She was in hell.

The ninth circle of hell and still walking. I need a sign. Please, God, I know I don't believe in you, but show me a goddamn sign. . . . I can say "goddamn" as much as I please; I'm in hell—thank you very much. You show me a way out, and I swear I'll change my ways. Just show me the way out. . . .

No reply. More heat. Talk about coming full circle. Back in foster care. Her uncle gone and her father gone. Her mother gone, Ella gone, Mary gone, Sam gone.

Sam. Oh, Jesus, Sam. . .

A shock of tears suddenly erupted from Gaia's eyes. She froze in the center of the sidewalk and dropped to one knee. She stared down at twenty years' worth of blackened chewing gum and shattered glass in the cracks of the pavement as her tears gathered on the ground.

I'm so sorry, Sam. I'm so sorry for everything I did to you. You know that, don't you? Please tell me you know that, wherever you are now. I can't think of you too often, Sam, because then the guilt. . . the guilt would be. . . but you understand that, don't you? You understand that there's a place for you—a separate place just for you that I've locked away in my brain and my heart that no one can ever touch—that I can't even touch, do you understand that? Are you listening, Sam? Can you help me off this street?

Legs swirled by her from every side, swiping her shoulders and her back.

"Goddamn druggies," someone spat.

"Get a job," somebody else barbed. Two boys howled with laughter.

She should have pounced on them. She should have jumped those asshole boys and ripped them apart. But she was too hot. And unless the sidewalk was going to give her a push, she wasn't capable of moving fast enough. She raised her head into the blur of colored lights and looked for a sign of any kind.

And then she saw one. Two, actually. The most beautiful signs she had ever seen. Two green signposts sticking out under the red streetlight just like it was Christmas.

Eighth Street and MacDougal Street.

It was a miracle. Eighth and MacDougal. Around the corner from Washington Square Park—the closest thing Gaia had to a home now. Somehow she'd guided herself home without even really knowing it. And Ed's was only a few more blocks from here. Maybe God had been listening?

She felt a burst of renewed energy and immediately broke into a jog, cutting across MacDougal Street and stumbling into the park like she'd just broken through the finishing tape of the New York City Marathon.

WASHINGTON SQUARE PARK HAD NEVER looked more beautiful. The trees rustled gloriously from the strong winds, and the arch was lit to perfection, shining like a bright white beacon signifying that Gaia had in fact made it home. It was

Personal Angel of Death

deserted but thoroughly unthreatening, as if all the skinheads and junkies had decided to give the Village bohemians and the NYU students a much-needed night off.

The chess tables were empty at this time of night, but they were the ultimate sight for Gaia's painfully sore eyes. She stumbled to the tables, plopped herself down on a stone seat, and slid her hands back and forth across the board, savoring the tactile taste of the familiar.

"Gaia. . ."

"Ed?" Gaia popped her head up from the table. Someone had whispered her name. She hoped that perhaps Ed had come to her, understanding through deep emotional telepathy that her legs and feet were nearly out of commission and that he needed to meet her halfway. She looked around her, searching through the round bushes and the angular branches of the trees, but there was no sign of Ed.

"Gaia," the voice whispered again. "Please."

The whispers were anxious and short of breath. She didn't know how she could have thought it was Ed. It was a girl's voice. A girl in trouble. Perhaps not every park-dwelling scumbag had gotten the memo about taking the night off. Gaia's spine snapped to attention as she pricked up her ears like a predator and chased down the voice with her eyes.

There, in the clearing by the brick rest rooms. A young woman's form shivered in silhouette as her hands reached out to Gaia, beckoning her with quick snaps of her wrists. "Jesus, hurry," the girl moaned.

Gaia didn't waste another moment. She jumped from her stone seat and raced toward the desperate voice, cranking every ounce of energy out of her wobbly legs, leaping two park benches and landing with a flat thud on the higher level of the park.

"I can't see you," Gaia said through deep, winded breaths. She staggered the rest of the way toward the voice. She'd forgotten just how painfully tired her muscles were. She hardly had the energy to be a hero. But her old instincts were still intact, and that was encouraging. Whatever Loki had done to her, her obsessive savior complex was still fully functional. "Come into the light where I can see you," she said.

The girl did as Gaia asked and stepped into a spike of light that cut through the branches from the street-lamps outside the park.

But when Gaia saw the face, her chest went numb. Every ounce of strength that was left in her heart began to crumble.

The vision of fiery red hair seemed to melt what was left of Gaia's defenses. Long, tangled red hair. Red velvet lips. A curvy form in a skintight black miniskirt and a black Nirvana T-shirt. . . There was no way she could be standing there, yet she was. These two basic truths were in such pure contradiction, Gaia wasn't even sure what to think. So she simply chose the truth that made her happier. The impossible one.

"Mary?"

"Gaia, hold on to me, okay?" Mary Moss begged meekly. She was shivering hard and holding on to her stomach.

Gaia was motionless and speechless. Her brain was still in a holding pattern, trying to wrap itself around this impossible encounter.

"My stomach," Mary complained. "My stomach feels like it's going to explode. I think I'm hurt bad. Hold me up."

Mary began to collapse. Gaia thrust her arms under Mary's to give her support. Once she had touched her, once she could feel how real she was, a huge wave of elation was unlocked. She wrapped her arms tightly around Mary and took deep inhalations of her spiced rose perfume.

"Mary, I don't get it," Gaia whispered into her ear, wetting her thick red hair with tears. "How is this happening?"

"I've missed you so badly," Mary said, breathing out with exhaustion as she gripped Gaia's shoulders. "So badly, it hurts. I wish you hadn't let me die. I wish you'd saved me."

Gaia pulled away, stunned and appalled. "What did you say?"

"You heard me," Mary said, wrapping her arms tightly around her midsection, cringing. "You know you could have gotten to me in time. You could have saved my life. But you didn't."

The words seemed to hover over Gaia's ears, forming a chain that wrapped around her neck like a cold steel noose and hanged her from the trees. "Don't say that," she begged in the near silence. She was choking on every word, gasping for a decent breath. "Please don't say that."

"Then save me this time," Mary moaned urgently. "*Please.* Don't let it happen again."

Suddenly Mary's entire body arched backward into a rigid pose of sheer agony. She let out a protracted rattling scream as the tip of a blade jutted straight through the center of her stomach. Gaia's eyes darted down to the knife, only to see it pulled out of Mary's stomach and plunged back through her again. And again.

It had happened so quickly. Instantaneously. Without any warning. Gaia was left frozen in place, her feet nailed to the ground as she watched Mary dying right before her eyes. There had been no time for action in this lightning-quick moment. No time for anything but shock.

Mary lurched forward, grasping at her wounds with one hand and flailing the other hand out, trying to latch onto Gaia's arm. Gaia grabbed Mary's hand and squeezed it as tightly as she could, kneeling to the ground with Mary as she doubled over.

"I'm so sorry, Mary," she whispered. She didn't know what else to say. She barely even understood what she was witnessing. All she knew was that somehow she'd failed again. Once again Gaia had only looked on and watched as her best friend was murdered.

Mary didn't speak a word. She glued her pleading eyes to Gaia's as blood trickled from her mouth, and then she collapsed in a heap on the grassy rocks.

Gaia let out a loud, involuntary blip of a scream, but it was cut short. Cut short by what she saw next. The man who had been standing behind Mary, holding the knife. Somehow Gaia hadn't even considered him until she looked up at his face.

The face with the vacant blue eyes and the shiny, sadistic grin. The face of the apparently immortal Josh Kendall.

Of course. Why would it be anybody else? Josh was the Grim Reaper. Gaia's own personal angel of death, tag teaming with Loki to kill anyone she loved.

"What do you see, Gaia?" he asked cryptically, maintaining his smile as he held the knife to Gaia's face. "You want to tell me who you were just talking to?" He hesitated for a moment, searching Gaia's eyes curiously. His question made no sense to her. Not that she would have answered him, anyway. She was too busy assessing the wisest way to kill him. He might have somehow survived a gunshot to the head, but that was nothing compared to what Gaia could do to him.

Josh lunged at her with the knife. Gaia hadn't expected it. He lunged hard and fast, aiming straight for her chest.

She felt her heart lurch at the swing of his knife. Yet another in this new flood of alien experiences. The unexpected shock to her system left the slightest gap in her reflex time. It was enough of a delay for Josh to nick her shoulder, but Gaia managed to dodge more serious injury, latching onto his arm and flipping him hard against the grassy rocks. The wicked landing knocked him out cold, and Gaia dove back down next to Mary.

Only there was no Mary. Mary was gone. Her body had melted into the bushes. Another living nightmare, like her mother? But she'd seemed so real. The confusion was piling on so quickly, Gaia could hardly keep track of what had confused her in the first place.

"Gaia. . . Help me. . ."

Oh God, not another voice.

He groaned in pain from behind her. But this voice she knew instantly. *His* voice. The one she'd been working overtime to drive from her head every other minute. His beautiful voice was speaking to her now, strained and muted by suffering. "Gaia, I need you. . . ."

She wanted to turn around, but some part of her already knew she would regret it. She knew she would be permanently damaged by whatever she saw, whether he was real or not. But still, how could she not look? How could she possibly miss a chance to see him again? Even if he was a ghost.

That's what they had to be. All of them. Ghosts. Gaia was seeing ghosts. Apparitions of the people she'd killed with her own negligence or ignorance. They seemed to obey none of the laws of nature, but they were too real to be dreams. It made perfect sense. How could these poor souls possibly be at rest when they never should have died in the first place? They'd all died for one reason and one reason only. Gaia Moore. And all she had to offer for their deaths was a long list of useless apologies.

"Gaia, can you help me?" he begged again from behind her. "Will you look at me? Please."

She had no other choice. How could she deny him anything? Even if he was a ghost. She turned slowly toward his meek and desperate voice, and then she looked straight at him. His tormented image burned holes in her eyes. Her first impulse was to vomit.

Sam Moon's face was hollow and gray. His eyes and mouth were contorted with a look of unfathomable pain, like a living Rodin sculpture—an agonized, tortured soul. Smoke rose from the two black holes at the center of his chest as he reached his hand out to Gaia and fell to his knees.

"Gaia, please," he moaned. "Don't let them hurt me anymore."

Everyone has some limit for pain—some point at which the pain becomes so great that it can hardly be felt anymore. And looking at Sam Moon, both dead and alive at the same time, Gaia had reached her limit. She'd retreated from her own body into some underground emotional bunker, leaving only her frozen skin and bones to witness this horror. She couldn't speak to this ghost. To speak to this ghost would be to make it real, and that was something her heart simply refused to do.

Two more shots rang out, and Sam's body shook from the impact as he collapsed on the ground. And then. . . thank God. . . his body, like Mary's, disappeared.

Gaia dropped to the ground, hoping to touch what was left of his ghostly image, but she was given no time to mourn him. Two more shots rang out from a silencer as two thick holes erupted in the tree next to her face. And there was nothing supernatural about the shots. They were quite real. She turned just in time to see Josh Kendall marching toward her with his nine millimeter thrust out, firing again and again in a succession of whispered blasts.

Move, Gaia, move. Another frustrating delay in reaction time as she dodged the gratuitous spray of bullets, rolling to her right. She turned to the bushes to run for cover, but standing there in front of the bushes. . . was Josh Kendall. With his knife. *How the hell. . . ?* She turned right back around to escape him, but coming up fast from behind her still. . . was Josh Kendall. With his gun.

Gaia looked in front of her and behind her again, and then she froze. Complete paralysis from head to toe.

Two of them. Two Joshes. One with a knife and one with a gun. *Okay, now I'm hallucinating. Or else I'm seeing more ghosts.*

Maybe Josh Kendall was haunting her. . . . *No way.* But if Josh was a ghost, then why were there still bullet holes in the trees? And why was her shoulder still bleeding from where he'd cut her?

But if they weren't ghosts, then what rational explanation could that leave? Other than the most obvious answer: Gaia had finally lost her mind. She'd been traumatized to her limit, and now she'd finally cracked. Maybe that's what it took for her to feel fear. A full-on psychotic break.

And apparently her psychosis had done the trick because as the two Joshes closed in on her, she began to feel something that was probably in the realm of terrified. She was unable to stave off the panic now. Unable to breathe or focus. She could barely move. It was taking control of her. She couldn't suppress that heart-racing hollow buzzing.

Josh took another swipe at her with the knife, and

once again Gaia barely reacted in time. She ducked under him awkwardly and rolled away, but gunshots were raining on her the moment she recovered. From the *other* Josh's gun.

Her heart was beating so hard, it seemed to be trying to pound its way out of her chest. She was breaking down from her breakdown. *Jesus, what now?* She had to do something. She had to conjure up some vestige of her former self. She had to at least rid him of that gun, or she was dead for sure.

She reached deep down into all her years of training and whatever was left of her spirit and launched into a flying kick. She snapped her leg out at the pistol, kicking it high out of Josh's hand somewhere into the bushes, and then tucked her body into a cannonball, rocketing straight into his body and knocking him into the dirt. The two tussled wildly on the ground until Gaia suddenly felt two strong hands grab the back of her shirt and yank her back up. She spun around to take him on, but when she saw his face, she felt the remainder of her infinitesimal hope fizzle.

Square jaw. Blue eyes. Cruel smile.

Now there were three.

Gun-toting Josh was on the ground. Knife-wielding Josh was standing next to him. *This* Josh was holding her tightly by her shirt. He might not have a weapon, but the mere fact of his existence was enough to leave

Gaia devastated, without an ounce of fight left in her. Her own delusions were trying to kill her. How could she fight her own delusions? How could she take on her own insanity? How could she do anything when she was pathetically quaking in her boots?

Welcome to your new life. Your new "normal" life.

Why had she agreed to that injection? That was the main question. Why would anyone in her right mind ask for this sensation? If this was fear, then fear made every move impossible. Fights had always been like chess games to her—planned methodical attacks, knowing the next five moves before the first. They were nothing but games, target practice. But this. . .

This was pathetic.

She didn't even raise her arms to fight now. She had nothing left to offer. No wits. Her mind was obviously gone. No confidence. She'd practically forgotten how to fight. And most of all, no bravery. It seemed her newfound dementia had stripped her of all her noble impulses and left her with only one very feeble impulse. The need to retreat.

So that was just what she did. Like a true coward, she ducked between her delusions and took off with whatever energy she had left. She didn't even dare to look back.

And so it was official. She was running from a

fight. For the first time in her life, Gaia Moore had chickened out. If this was what fear felt like, she should have just chosen death in the first place.

DON'T GO TO THE DOOR, YOU LOSER.

Ed had already made that mistake six times today, and he was thoroughly sick of himself. He'd heard phantom knocks at the door, phantom phones ringing

Foulmouthed Angel

from the other room. . . . She was never there.

He twisted himself uncomfortably in his bed and wrapped his rubbery pillow around his ears. That was definitely *not* a knock at the front door he'd just heard. He'd learned that much after this heartbreaking, interminable day. If he had to hear himself call out her name to an empty hallway once more or whisper it hopefully into a dead phone line, he would. . .

He didn't know what he'd do. Something self-destructive. Something to punish himself for his idiotic optimism.

It was his own fault. All those months working

with Brian, the world's first physical therapist/professional wrestler/inspirational speaker. Ed had spent so many weeks listening to Brian, trying to get back on his feet with "the power of positive thinking," he'd ended up falling prey to the worst kind of blind optimism. "Anything is possible if you just put your mind to it" and all that crap. Nothing could be further from the truth. It might be true of recovering calf muscles, but it had nothing to do with human emotion.

Going from a paraplegic to a biped was one thing.

But try losing the love of your life after only one kiss, Brian. Try confessing months of unrequited love to her and then watching her disappear—for God knows what reason. She may have died some horrific, tragic death. Or she may have just had the simple realization that she never cared about you to begin with, even after you'd poured your heart out to her. Try being stuck in that little ring of hell—missing her, hating her, mourning her, loving her all at the same time, knowing you'll probably never get any answers or see her again. Try that, Brian, and then tell me what's left of your godforsaken optimism.

Ed heard another knock at the door. But it was more than a knock this time. It was a full-force pounding, loud enough to cut through his pillow-smothered hearing. His torso shot up on the bed as his head snapped toward the quick, insistent thuds coming from outside.

It's her. Jesus Christ, it's her. You're a genius, Brian. You're a goddamn genius!

Ed practically fell from the bed as he pulled a crumpled T-shirt from the floor, tugged it over his head, hoisted himself up on his crutches, and hobbled out of his room—straight to the front door as the knock grew louder and louder.

He hesitated for a moment, pressing his cheek to the door as his hand crushed the brass knob. This would be the last time he would do it. He couldn't possibly handle another disappointment. If he heard any other voice but hers come through that door, it would be the last straw. Whatever the hell that meant.

"Gaia. . . ?" he uttered tentatively.

"Open the goddamn door!" She groaned.

It was the most beautiful demand Ed had ever heard. The foulmouthed angel herself sent straight from heaven.

Ed ripped open the door. Gaia fell into his arms before he'd even gotten his first word out. She clenched the back of his shirt in her hands and buried her head between his neck and shoulder. Still not a word spoken between them. Her head felt like a hot compress that had just been doused in boiling water. Unless she'd stuck her head in the oven for the last hour, she must have a massive fever.

His immediate impulse was to get her to a chair or a couch or a bed. But first, at least for a moment, he had to give in to his more selfish impulse: the need to hold her and to feel her holding him. He'd convinced himself that this sensation was only going to exist in memories, so to actually feel her in his arms again was one of those minor miracles that needed to be at least temporarily savored.

Gaia had kept her promise. She'd told him she would be back, and she'd just proved what Ed had always known. Gaia wasn't a liar. An old saying popped into Ed's head as he held on to her, although he couldn't remember all of it. *If you love something, set it free. If it comes back. . .* He couldn't remember the rest. He'd remember later, when he could think of anything other than Gaia Moore.

Finally he forced his nobler instincts to return. He loosened his grip and tried to move her farther into the living room, where she could at least sit down, but Gaia was clearly not ready to move. She held her ground and clung tightly to him like a small child clinging to her father's leg at the doctor's office. It was so bizarrely out of character. Gaia never feared anything, nor did she ever act like a child. Unless you counted her love of Froot Loops.

"Are you okay?" he asked gently, his mouth only a half inch from her ear.

She didn't respond. She only tightened her embrace.

"What is it?" he asked. "What happened?"

"I'm so glad you're here," she breathed.

"You have *no idea*," Ed replied, letting his lips graze her earlobe. He had much more to say to her. But he sensed that what she needed right now was just his embrace and a fair amount of silence. "You're burning up," he said. "I think you should lie down."

"I think you're right," she said. Her entire body began to give, leaning more and more on Ed's right arm to support her weight.

He helped her to his room, gingerly holding her up with his right arm and holding himself up with his left crutch. The trip took about five times as long as it should have, but Ed luxuriated in each additional moment that she allowed him to support her.

They made it to his room, and Gaia collapsed on his bed. It was actually the first time he'd seen her from any distance, and the sight of her caused a twinge of pain in his chest. Her face was gaunt and washed out. Her hair was so matted with sweat, it had turned dark brown. Her eyes were red and glazed over from fever, and her lips were so pale, they were nearly invisible. She looked like she was just waiting for the detectives to outline her in chalk.

He leaned over and carefully shifted the pillow so that her head could rest more comfortably. She seemed too weak to even lift her head to assist him.

"Gaia. . . ?" Ed couldn't even tell if she could hear him, but he needed at least a few answers. The initial burst of joy at seeing her alive had quickly worn off. It was replaced by the shock and confusion of seeing her looking closer to dead. "Gaia, what *happened* to you?" he asked. "Is Sam all right? Did you find him?"

"I can't talk about that now," she croaked.

"Well, what the hell happened last night? Who did this to—"

"Can we *not* go there right now?" she insisted. She was lying still with her eyes closed, but her immense pain was visible even with her face at rest. "Can you just hold on to me for a little bit? Just until I catch my breath?"

Ed was too stunned to respond. *Hold on to me?* It was the most un-Gaia-like request he had ever heard. Gaia was asking *him* to hold *her*. *She* was asking *him*.

But he knew not to hesitate for too long. He figured he had about five seconds to spare until she would shut him out. This was no time for second guessing and self-doubt. In spite of his twenty-four hours of frustration and yearning, somehow tonight Gaia needed him even more than he needed her. Could he hold on to her for a little bit?

"I can do that," he said.

He carefully lowered the bars on the left side of his hospital bed and then climbed in as gently as he could, trying to leave Gaia as much space as she needed. He lay down on his back, not even sure what to do with his

131

right arm as he kept his eyes on her pained expression.

Gaia turned over on her side and nestled her head on his shoulder, breathing hot, shallow breaths into his neck. Her position cued him to wrap his arm around her, which he did, gripping her shoulder tightly as she clenched the chest area of his T-shirt in her hand.

The moment they settled into each other, Gaia's breaths began to slow down, bit by bit until she was nearly silent.

"Are you okay?" Ed whispered, keeping his body as still as he could for her, his eyes fixed on the ceiling.

"Better," she whispered, sounding half asleep already. "This is better."

A few seconds more and she was fast asleep.

Ed took a deep, cathartic breath and closed his eyes. He couldn't quite fathom how much had changed in the last five minutes. But he agreed with Gaia. Things were suddenly much, much better. Optimism. . . *Genius, Brian. You're a goddamn genius.*

He tried once more to remember that old saying as he drifted toward sleep.

If you love something, set it free. If it comes back. . .

If it comes back. . .

He didn't really care what the rest of it was. Gaia had come back, and that was enough.

To: L
From: QR2

   Test completed. Serum seems effective.
Indications of hallucination confirmed.
Indications of paranoia still unknown. Subject
performed below usual skill level. Displayed certain indications of fear in the forms of tentative action and retreat, but nothing conclusive.

To: QR2
From: L

  Continue as planned and provide further
details in next report. We are dealing with certain unknowns. We cannot pinpoint with any cer-
tainty if and when the serum has taken full
effect or when it will wear off. Monitor closely.
   New field agent is on board. Full access to
Enigma and subject should be secured within the week.

Her request
that he hold
her last
night—another
anomalous
moment
born out **so**
of her **busted**
desperation
and a very
high fever.

HER BEAUTY WAS A MAJOR DIS-

Conversing with Thin Air

traction. Not to mention her subtle resemblance to Katia. It was making Tom sick with guilt. He had dire and immediate issues to deal with: Gaia's questionable health and safety, Loki's slippery maneuvers and vengeful intentions. These had been Tom's obsessions for the last five years, and if anything, he'd planned to make them even greater obsessions as of the last forty-eight hours. So why could he not stop staring at her oversized brown eyes?

At 7 A.M. Natasha had called for an early briefing at Odessa, a small Russian diner on Avenue A. Apparently a great deal had happened since their last meeting at the seaport, and Tom had started demanding details before she'd even brought her coffee to her lips.

"There was a skirmish of some kind," Natasha said, sipping carefully and then placing the cup back on its saucer.

"Skirmish? What kind of skirmish?"

"We're not altogether sure," she replied cautiously. "Agents were of course keeping their distance, and it was quite dark in the park. They were surrounded by bushes. . . ."

"*Who?* Who was surrounded by bushes?" Natasha's

hesitation was only making Tom more anxious. "How many assailants were there?"

Natasha averted her gaze from Tom's eyes, tucking her silken, honey-colored hair behind her ear with one delicate finger. "That is what we are not sure of," she said. "There was at least one, or there may have been three. . . maybe even five."

"How is that possible?" Tom demanded. "How obstructed were their sight lines?"

"We had two agents, gathering as much as they could through the bushes," she said defensively. "But when the battle fell into view, they could not confirm if she was fighting different men. . . or if they were all the same man."

"I don't understand—"

"And sometimes, Tom," she interrupted. "I'm sorry. . . but sometimes. . . she seemed to be jumping at nothing. Or conversing with thin air." Natasha quickly looked down at her coffee and took another long, slow sip.

Still hallucinating. His daughter was still being tormented by visions of God knew what. The thought of it brought excruciating pressure to the back of his head.

Each new report served only as another challenge to Tom's strictly enforced morality. Because he knew his brother had done something to her. Something chemical and inhuman. And Tom could feel himself crossing over into impulses much darker than just the need to protect Gaia. He was beginning to share in his brother's need for vengeance. He shook it off as best he could.

"Where is she now?" he asked quietly.

"She did not come home last night," Natasha said. "She spent the night at Ed Fargo's."

Tom flashed Natasha a disapproving glare. He couldn't mask his disappointment with her. It had been less than forty-eight hours since Gaia had been *kidnapped* from that very location. Ed was Gaia's closest friend, and Tom respected that. He understood that she must have needed a true confidant and a familiar face very badly after all she'd been through, but Ed Fargo's apartment was far from a safe haven now. If Loki was looking for her, Ed's would be the first place he'd go.

"Well, you have to get her out of there," Tom stated severely. He dispensed with the need for any further explanation. "You have to get her out of there today."

Natasha seemed caught off guard by his harsh words. She bowed her head slightly and then straightened her posture. "I understand," she replied. "Of course. I will do it this morning."

"She needs to stay *home*," Tom implored her. "With *you*. You need to earn her trust, Natasha. That's essential to keeping her safe."

"Of course, you're right, Tom," she said. Suddenly her eyes were overflowing with heartfelt contrition. "You are absolutely right."

Tom lightened up his expression, hoping he hadn't been too hard on her. "I'm sorry," he muttered to the tabletop, shaking his head. "I don't mean to take it out on you." He turned back to her and looked into those overpowering brown eyes again. "You have to understand. . . . I've been trying for years to figure out the best way to protect her, and I just haven't been able—"

"It is *okay*," she interrupted him.

Tom knew she had interrupted him just to spare him any further self-flagellation. That seemed to be the kind of compassionate heart she had.

She slid her coffee to the side and reached across the table, placing her gentle hands over Tom's. Tom felt his hands go rigid, just as his whole body had the night before when she'd touched his shoulder.

But this time he didn't pull away.

"I will try my best, Tom," she said, her eyes charged with sincerity. "I will try to be as *motherly* as I can to her. I promise you. I want for her to trust me as much as you do. I hope. . ." She dropped her eyes to the table.

"What?" Tom asked, lowering his head slightly to regain eye contact. "What were you going to say?"

"I. . . ," she began, locking her eyes with his again. "I hope also that *you* trust me, Tom. You do, do you not?"

Tom looked into her eyes and wondered how she had done it. How she had managed to be an agent all these years and still have such a living, breathing heart. There was no hardened facade, no cold, brittle membrane that blocked all her genuine emotions from being outwardly expressed. Tom had thought the "emotional wall" was practically standard issue at the Agency. It came with the badge and the gun. But somehow she'd avoided it. She really was a rare breed. Rare and disconcertingly beautiful.

"I do," Tom stated simply, his eyes fixed securely to hers. "I do trust you."

Natasha unleashed a bright smile that caught Tom totally off guard. It caused a most unexpected prickling sensation to run down the center of his chest. Some unknowable amount of time passed as the two of them stayed frozen in the exact same position.

Something about her smile. . . No, it wasn't the smile itself. But something about the way the smile made Tom feel reminded him so much of. . .

Tom suddenly tugged his hands out from under hers, rattling the two cups of coffee on the table as he cut the invisible adhesive between their eyes.

"I'm sorry," Natasha uttered senselessly as she abruptly busied her hands. She smoothed her hair back and her dress down.

"No, no," Tom mumbled uncomfortably, making unnecessary adjustments to his coffee cup. "N-No, I was just thinking. . . ," he stammered, looking any-where other than at her. "I really think you'd better go pick up Gaia."

"Yes, of course," she replied, overlapping him. "Of course. I will do this right now."

Natasha slid out of the booth and struggled to get her coat on quickly. "I will contact you the moment she's been secured."

"Good," Tom said. "Perfect."

Natasha walked briskly to the door and quickly disappeared from the window. Tom turned back to the table and tried not to think.

IT HAD BEEN FIVE YEARS SINCE

this particular phenomenon had occurred.

Gaia had gotten fully accustomed to having no idea where she was for the first two minutes of any and every morning. It was an inherent part of her daily ritual: Wait for her vision to unblur, feel around the bed for clues, blind herself with sunlight or a bedside lamp until she could see the room, and then. . . *Right, still here. Same life, Gaia. Sorry, try again tomorrow.*

But this morning was different. It seemed like for the first time in years, Gaia knew where she was from the moment her eyes had begun to open.

She was in Ed's bedroom. Resting her head on his chest. And she felt better.

So much better.

Maybe her fever had broken. Maybe she was through with her painful visions and nightmares. It was as if Ed himself possessed some sort of magical healing qualities. Why not? He'd found some miraculous way to bring back the use of his legs. Maybe he'd found some miraculous way to heal Gaia overnight while they were sleeping. She'd felt it from the moment she grabbed his shirt and lay down on his shoulder the night before. Her breathing had immediately begun to return to her. The nauseating, fearlike feeling began to subside. She began to remember who she was.

It was as if the rest of the world was on some mission to unravel her—to hammer away at her identity until there was no Gaia left in Gaia. But Ed always seemed to do just the opposite. Ed always seemed to be keeping her intact. Reminding her of who she was in her weakest moments. Letting her be who she was when she was strong. He was a healer. There was no other explanation.

She rolled her eyes upward toward his chin to be sure he was still asleep. She was extremely careful not to move her head. If she moved her head, then she might wake him. And then she'd have to move from this perfect position—his chest as her pillow and his hand firmly grasping her shoulder. She couldn't have him wake up and find her like this. It would just be too obvious. . . too close. A sudden wave of agitation washed over her, constricting her chest and tensing up her hands.

What did that mean, "too close"? *What* would be too obvious?

Gaia. . . enough already. Your denial has reached joke status. You have an IQ on the genius level. You know what you're feeling. No amount of guilt or confusion is going to change what you already know.

She felt awfully tired of herself, lying so happily in Ed's embrace. Tired of pretending this thing hadn't happened. This change in her feelings for Ed. Ed had the courage to tell her everything he was feeling. Everything he'd always been feeling. He was the fearless one now. She was just plain chicken. That injection must really have worked. Because here she was, as safe, sound, and happy as she would probably ever feel, and she was too cowardly to move a muscle.

Maybe now was the time to test out a little bravery again. Yes. Now was the time to let herself give in to an irresistible impulse she'd been having since she'd opened her eyes. A small but dangerously telling impulse. . .

Absolutely. Why not? She had nothing to be afraid of.

Ed was still asleep.

She'd just do it very slowly and very gently.

She surveyed the landscape of his torso, checking twice more to be sure that his diaphragm was rising and falling with the regularity of sleep. And then, as cautiously as if she were defusing a bomb, Gaia stretched her hand out wider on his T-shirt. *Here goes nothing.* She slid her fingers slowly across his chest, and then she grabbed on firmly to his side. Success. Mission accomplished. Now she was holding him. Now they were holding each other.

You see? There's really nothing "frightening" about this. Brave is easy.

Ed suddenly shifted slightly in the bed.

Damn. He's awake.

Gaia slammed her eyes shut and froze every muscle in her body, quickly faking as much fake sleep as she could.

Fake sleeping? Nice, Gaia. Brave. Very brave.

ACCIDENTS. HE COULD ALWAYS CHALK

Too Intimate

it up to accidents and extenuating circumstances. Ed had awoken to his sunlit ceiling, the low-pitched din of New York morning traffic wafting through the window, and he'd realized that Gaia's head was now resting on his chest. But only because she was sound asleep.

Just an accident of sleep, he was sure. Another random occurrence that indicated no actual desire on Gaia's part. Like their one real kiss—just this anomalous moment born only out of heated and totally chaotic circumstances. Or her request that he hold her last night—another anomalous moment born out of her desperation and a very high fever. Never really an act of her will. Never simply because she wanted it.

It wasn't doing wonders for Ed's ego. Still, Ed did everything in his power not to move an inch. He didn't want to wake her. Even if her position was an accident, waking up with Gaia's head on his chest was still an easy number one on his Top Ten Stellar Ways to Greet the Morning. At least she was there and not gone. At least she was alive and not dead. At least she was safe and in his arms. . . . That was worth plenty, no matter what the reason.

Gaia shifted her hand slightly on his chest. It sent a wave of remarkable shivers down his spine.

Accidents, Ed. Just accidents. . .

Only her hand didn't stop moving. It spread out flat, pressing its fingers firmly against the center of his chest. And then it glided ever so slowly. Across the entire width of his torso, firing off every nerve ending from his throat through to his fingertips. And it was *still moving. . .* Her hand finally anchored just under his ribs, grasping firmly the muscles of his waist.

Unless Ed was hallucinating, Gaia had just caressed his chest and reached over to hold him. One very clear and concise thought erupted in his head.

That was not an accident.

No way. It was too slow. Too deliberate to be a midsleep flop of the arm. Too intimate to be some childlike teddy-bear-substitution maneuver. It was a clear-cut, undeniably *intentional,* dare he even say *sexually charged,* gesture. Last night she'd asked him to hold her. But this morning. . . *she* wanted to hold *him.* And that was something completely different.

Could physical contact still be an anomaly after the third incidence? Ed thought not. The third time wasn't just a charm. It was one hundred percent *antianomalous.* Ed's heart rate doubled. A thick dose of primitive joy began to pulse through his veins in the form of pure adrenaline. He'd been doing everything humanly possible to stay completely still, but he couldn't help himself. His sudden rush forced him to shift slightly in the bed.

When he settled again, Gaia's hand had thankfully still not moved.

Wait. Was that a good thing? Why hadn't she moved at all? Was she still asleep? Oh, Jesus, if she was still asleep, then this was all meaningless. *Don't let her be asleep. Please don't let her be asleep.* He crunched his neck forward, trying to see if Gaia's eyes were still closed.

And they were. Sealed shut. Fast asleep. Ed's heart quickly sank down to somewhere under the bed. *Let it go, Ed. Just let it go.*

She was probably dreaming. She could be dreaming about anyone or anything. She could be dreaming about Sam for all he knew. Still, he couldn't help watching her face as she slept.

HE COULDN'T BE LOOKING ANYMORE.

It had to be safe to cut the make-believe-sleep routine.

Cheesy Love Stories

Gaia opened her eyes. And when she did, she was looking directly into the wide-open eyes of Ed Fargo. He was most definitely still looking. And although Ed might have been caught staring at her, Gaia had just been caught gripping his waist and feigning sleep. So busted. So tragically busted.

"You're awake," she croaked. *Brilliant observation, Gaia.* She was sure she was blushing.

"You are, too," he said. An impish smile spread across his face.

Gaia felt compelled to hide her head somewhere.

She racked her brains for some ludicrous explanation or excuse as to why she might be grabbing his waist. Why she might be pretending to be asleep. *My, aren't we full of bravery this morning?* The only thing was, after a few seconds longer in his arms and Gaia no longer felt like she needed to be brave. Excuses no longer seemed necessary. She began to feel quite unexpectedly. . . comfortable.

It soon became clear that in spite of their mutually embarrassing discoveries, neither one of them planned to budge from their position. Gaia didn't remove her hand from his waist, nor did he remove his from her shoulder. The only movement on either of their parts was to adjust their heads so as to see each other better. Gaia shifted her head up to his shoulder, and Ed tilted his head down from his pillow.

Now that they were face-to-face. . . there was just something oddly natural about their physical configuration. Gaia suddenly remembered that he was Ed. Ed Fargo. The one remaining life-form she could trust. And finally Gaia realized the truth. The fact that he was Ed Fargo could make their closeness *more* comfortable rather than less. Even their extended silence felt totally comfortable. Serene, even.

Gaia couldn't tell whether allowing herself to be this close was fearless or brave. She only knew that she had no desire to change it.

"Are you feeling better?" Ed asked.

"I am," she said, checking again through her body to see if she agreed with her statement. "I think the fever's gone."

"I'm glad." Ed sighed. "You looked touch-and-go there for a minute. It was kind of freaky."

"Try feeling it," she said.

Another long, comfortable silence as their eyes relaxed into permanent contact. Everything was suddenly falling into place.

"I really didn't think you were coming back," he said, turning slightly on his side.

"Why? I promised I would come back," she said matter-of-factly, adjusting her head so that their faces were in even closer proximity.

"You did, didn't you?" He smiled, inching his face a bit closer to hers. Whatever she was doing, Ed was doing it, too. And she didn't want to stop him.

He let his eyes roam over her entire face, brushing a few of the matted hairs away from her mouth and then giving her eyes his full attention again. "If I said something along the lines of, 'I was losing my mind without you,' do you think that would be over the top?"

"Yes," she said definitively, tracing the way his wild hair crushed against his pillow. "That would be just as bad as me saying something like, 'You were the only thing that kept me going last night.'"

Faces an inch closer.

"That doesn't sound so bad to me," Ed noted.

"Yeah, well, you've seen a lot more movies than I have. You've been totally desensitized to `cheesy love stories`." Close enough to see the flecks of gold in his pupils. Close enough to feel his breath against her cheek and see each dark individual fleck of stubble.

"Is this a cheesy love story?" he asked.

"Could you say anything *more* 'cheesy love story' than that?"

"I don't know. Could your face be any closer to mine without kissing me?"

Gaia froze at this statement. She swore she could hear the screeching rubber of a car slamming on the brakes somewhere off in the distance. Ed's smile dropped away instantly. He must have thought he'd just said the *wrong* thing. The silence that followed wasn't one of those comfortable ones. But she only stayed frozen for a moment. Because she was so unbelievably tired of being frozen. And dishonest. With herself and Ed. Frozen wasn't really how she felt at all.

"Actually, I think, probably. . ." She shifted herself even closer to Ed. "Probably I've got at least another. . ." Ed's smile began to reappear in the corner of his mouth. She moved her face even closer until the tip of her nose had passed the tip of his. "Okay, there," she said without a hint of a smile, grazing his strong chin with her own. "I knew I had more room."

Ed cupped his sizable hand behind her head and ran his finger gently along the back of her ear. He made sure to match her deadpan expression. "You always have to be right, don't you?"

The sudden pounding at Ed's front door snapped Gaia backward. It was echoing through her head—like one of those `infernal New York City jackhammers`.

"Jesus, who is that?" Gaia backed herself up against the headboard.

Ed's face washed over with puzzlement as he stared at Gaia. "It's just the door. . . ," he said.

They wouldn't stop pounding. Pounding as if they were trying to break the damn thing down. Sinister images from the other side of that door were flashing through Gaia's head like lightning. She could actually see them. Like psychic visions, she could see them. All of the Joshes waiting on the other side of that door. Waiting for Ed to crack that door open so they could break through with their silencers and their hunting knives and punch an endless amount of bloody holes in Ed like they'd done to Mary. Like they'd done to Sam. Ed was all she had left in the world, and now they were going to take him and gouge out his eyes and leave his hollow body on the living-room floor. The angels of death, following her no matter where she went.

Ed grabbed for his crutches, but Gaia tugged him back to the bed. "You can't go out there, Ed, get it? Do *not* answer that door."

Ed gave her that strange look again. "Gaia, what the

hell is wrong with you? It's just the door. It's probably a FedEx for my folks or something. Relax. I'm just going to see who it is."

"Ed, don't. Can't you hear the way they're pounding out there?"

"Gaia, they've knocked twice gently. What are you talking about?"

"They're *murderers*, Ed. Cold-blooded murderers. And they're here to kill us both."

Ed's expression changed from puzzled to something much more along the lines of deeply concerned. He leaned back to her and placed his hand on her forehead. "I want you to lie down, okay?" he said. "I think maybe that fever is acting up. I'll be right back."

"Don't," she begged one last time. "Please don't."

But it was no use. Ed was already out the door. He was already gone.

How could anyone in his right mind deny that there is a force on this earth greater than ourselves? I've never understood that. Don't get me wrong, I have the utmost respect for the existentialists. But let's be honest. They're only telling a part of the story. Because if we really bear the sole responsibility for all our choices and actions in life, then how on earth do you explain "chemistry"?

Chemistry between two people. It's simply not something we choose. It chooses us. What man or woman hasn't felt that indescribable electric connection after sharing only a few sentences with a complete stranger? Or even with someone who, for all rational reasons, they should despise?

We can't be held culpable for these uninvited electric connections. We can't be. Because if we were, then I would have to give in to the mountain of guilt

that's threatening to come tumbling down on me like an
avalanche at any moment.

What is this undeniable electricity with Natasha? I can't
understand it, and controlling it
has grown more difficult in only
a day's time. All I find myself
wanting to do is apologize.

To you, Katia. I feel this
overwhelming need to apologize to
you for this connection I have
not even asked for or created. Do
you think perhaps she's some kind
of substitute for you? A substitute mother to Gaia, a distant
member of your family? Could that
explain the adolescent burning in
my chest when she smiles at me?
If it weren't for me, you and I
would still be together, and all
these selfish, inappropriate
questions would be moot.

That's what I feel right now,
Katia. Disgustingly selfish and
inappropriate. It's bad enough
that I would have these trivial
feelings that betray *you*—you, who
have been living in my heart and

my thoughts any moment I've
stopped to stand still. But to
let these feelings distract me
from *Gaia*—Gaia, who needs my
undivided attention now more than
ever—that, to me, feels unforgivable. Is it, Katia? Is this vague
feeling I'm having unforgivable?

God, I wish we could just go
back in time. Back to that first
moment in that little overstocked
Village bookstore when you and I
first met. First spoke. First
fell in love. Back to the brilliant simplicity of innocent
young love. Do you remember that
feeling? That feeling of knowing
you'd found something you never
wanted to give up? Of knowing
that at that moment, you were
exactly where you were supposed
to be? I miss that feeling,
Katia. I miss it very much.

She had more important things to worry about, anyway. Like whether

planet ed

she had set her VCR to tape tonight's "very special *Friends*."

"WHO IS IT?"

Heather was startled by the harshness of his tone. He sounded like he was growling. "Jesus, Ed, it's just Heather. Can you chill?"

Insulting Consolation

There was a long pause before she heard him unlatch the door. *God, was it that hard a decision?* He finally opened the door. But he didn't open it all the way. He stood in the doorway and held his arm behind the door, totally blocking her entry. Nice. How very inviting.

He looked like he'd just climbed out of bed. His hair was all piled up on one side, and the center of his T-shirt was totally crumpled up like he'd been clinging to it all night. He couldn't have looked any cuter. . . . It was a little depressing.

"Did you have any plans to go to school today?" she asked, looking him up and down and then checking her watch.

"Do you need something?" he asked impatiently.

Heather widened her eyes, making sure she'd made it clear how offensive his reply was. She waited a beat before speaking. "I see that you, and your hair, seem to have awoken on the wrong side of the bed this morning."

"Look, I had a really rough night, okay? I'm not trying to be rude. Can we talk later?"

"Oh, yeah," Heather said, crossing her arms. "That's *much less* rude."

"Heather." He groaned. "Come on."

She paused for a moment, trying to swallow how much it genuinely hurt to be brushed off this thoroughly. She couldn't believe this conversation was still taking place in Ed's *hallway*. Maybe he'd be a little kinder when he heard why she'd come. "Fine," she said, dropping her eyes. "I just wanted to know if you'd heard from Gaia yet. I wanted to know if she was okay."

"She's okay," Ed said. "Everything's okay now."

"Really?" Heather squeaked. Heather was still surprising herself with how genuine her own concern for Gaia had become in the last forty-eight hours. The news came as a real relief to her. "Have you seen her?"

"I have. Let's talk about this later—"

"Well, where is she now?" Heather asked.

Ed's eyes darted behind him for a split second. "She's here," he said.

"She is?" Heather found herself rising slightly on her tiptoes to see past Ed into the apartment.

Right at the end of his living room, at the corner of the hallway that led into his bedroom, was Gaia. She had a very odd expression on her face. Like she was either very frightened. . . or maybe confused. And although she was fully clothed, she, too, looked like she'd just climbed out of bed.

Heather felt nauseated. Or was it infuriated? Or

just incredibly sad? She looked into Ed's eyes. "Did she sleep over?" she asked, barely opening her mouth.

"Heather, can we talk later. . . ?"

She found herself searching Ed's eyes for any memory of the way the two of them used to be. Before this awful year. Before Gaia Moore existed. She found nothing.

Fine. That was fine. She had put her life on the line for Gaia, and now she hadn't even been granted apartment-entry privileges. She was struck with a nagging need to cry, but she wouldn't show an ounce of it to Ed or his new roommate. She'd turned over her new leaf. And she refused to be petty. No matter what.

"Well. . . ," she began, being sure to literally keep her chin up. "I thought maybe you guys could use some coffee." *Give him the big smile, Heather. The big smile.* "Do you guys want to stop at Starbucks with me before school?"

Ed looked back at Gaia. Heather could see her give him a quirky little smile. He turned back to the Heather in the hallway. "Maybe not this morning, okay?" He followed up his statement with the most insulting consolation smile.

Heather smiled right back, though—feeling like her face might crack. "Okay," she said, as intensely bubbly as she could muster. "I guess I'll just see you guys in school, then."

"Sounds good," Ed said, already beginning to close the door.

Heather turned toward the elevator and took a few steps, but she turned back. "I'm glad Gaia's okay."

The door was already closed. Fine. No problem. That was no problem.

She didn't let the tears flow until she'd gotten halfway down the block. She kept trying to remind herself of her new leaf as she approached Starbucks. She didn't want to resent Gaia, but God, wasn't she at least allowed to be jealous? Just flat-out envious? Envious of *any* love affair, for God's sake, not even just Ed and Gaia's?

Heather Gannis had never—repeat, *never*—gone this long without a boyfriend. Not since boys stopped being gross in the fourth grade. No, even then she'd had a boyfriend. Seth Weinstein.

But thanks to Gaia Moore—*not* that Heather was resentful, what with her new leaf—but thanks to Gaia, Heather had lost two boyfriends in a row. Now she couldn't even get her ex-boyfriend to go for coffee. Even if he could *bring* his new girlfriend. *That* was depressing.

Heather hurled her shoulder against the door of Starbucks and stepped up to the counter to order herself a double espresso. If she couldn't have a boyfriend, then at least she could have enough caffeine to make a buffalo stand up on two legs.

She tapped her foot impatiently at the pickup counter as she ran a continuous image of Gaia's quirky little smile through a mental loop. What did that smile mean? What was their little "special connection" all about, anyway? *New leaf, Heather. New leaf.* Who cared? Not Heather. She had more important things to worry about, anyway. Like whether she had set her VCR to tape tonight's "a very special *Friends*."

"Double espresso!" the Starbucks barker announced.

Heather snatched up her hot beverage, ripping the top off to get to that caffeine buzz ASAP.

But maybe she'd been a little too eager. Because when she ripped the top off, she proceeded to spill the entire boiling-hot cup directly onto another customer. Another extremely cute customer. To be more specific, on `the crotch of the extremely cute customer.`

"Oh my God, I am *so sorry.*"

The poor guy folded himself inward, trying to pull himself away from his own clothes. "It's okay," he said, laughing.

"I am *so, so sorry,*" she repeated at least four more times.

"It's fine," he assured her. "Please, I'm fine."

Heather grabbed a mile-high stack of napkins and ran at him. She thrust them toward the stain before remembering that she couldn't exactly wipe off that particular area. He laughed loudly as he made a few useless attempts to do something with the huge brown stain on his jeans. "Good aim," he joked.

"I guess so," she said nervously. "Oh God, I am—"

"Sooo sorry, I know," he said. "Have I by chance mentioned that it's *okay?*"

"Yes." Heather giggled, dropping her head in her hands, shamefaced. "Yes, I believe you have."

"Well, good," he said with a smile. No, not "a smile." More like *the* most heart-stopping smile Heather had ever seen. She wasn't even sure if she was giggling from embarrassment or just from pure schoolgirl awe at how drop-dead gorgeous he was. Everything about him. A face chiseled from stone. Jet black hair and crystal blue eyes. Taut biceps peeking out from his loose T-shirt.

"Look," she said, trying to avoid getting her eyes stuck on him in a trancelike state. "Obviously you have to at least let me pay for the cleaning bill."

"Cleaning bill? They're jeans. Please don't tell me you dry-clean your jeans."

"O-Okay. . . ," she stammered. "I don't know, then let me wash them for you."

"Now you're going to do my laundry?"

"Well. . . What can I do? Look, here's my number. Just call me with the bill, okay?"

Heather jotted down her name and number on a napkin and handed it to him.

"Ahhh," he exclaimed as he took the napkin. "You've caught on to my ingenious ploy to collect phone numbers from `beautiful, clumsy girls.`" He flashed her his smile again, and she felt her toes melting. Whole body soon to follow.

"Okay, whatever." Why had she regressed into the persona of a giggling twelve-year-old? Could it have something to do with the fact that he'd just called her beautiful? "I have to go, okay?"

"Where?" he asked.

Don't say to school. Do not say that you have to go to school.

"I just have to go," she said, trying to locate the door. He pointed it out to her. "Right, *that way*," she mumbled. "*Okay.* Okay, 'bye now. So call me about that bill, right." Heather spun around twice more before she finally made her way toward the door. She stopped once more. "And did I mention how *totally sorry* I was for—"

"It's *fine*," he interrupted, glimpsing the napkin with her number. "*Heather.* Don't worry about it, Heather. We are going to be *just fine.*"

"Okay," she agreed with a smile, taking one last look at his unreal face as she backed out the door.

She walked three full blocks in a daze before she realized she hadn't even asked him his name.

"I'M REALLY SORRY ABOUT BEFORE," Gaia said, keeping her eyes low as she poured her third bowl of Froot Loops. Thank God Ed was always fully stocked

A Nice Rubber Room

on Froot Loops, because they were just about her only solace right now, after that ludicrous freak-out with Ed's door. Obviously she'd been way too optimistic about the sudden disappearance of her symptoms. After all, it wouldn't be her life if it was that easy. She tried to do her own little therapy session in her head while Ed toasted himself an everything bagel.

The best she could come up with was this: It was kind of like someone who'd been blind their whole life regaining their sight. Or a deaf person getting one of those cochlear implants. The shapes must look so totally insane to the blind person at first. The sounds must be so loud to the deaf person. If you'd grown up only knowing nothing, wouldn't even the smallest thing seem like too much? At least at first? That had to be what was happening with her fear response. Gaia was so unaccustomed to being startled that now everything was startling. Her introduction to being startled just felt like a terrifying nightmare.

That was one theory. The other was that she'd lost her freaking mind.

Crunch, crunch. Don't look at Ed.

"Gaia, you don't need to be sorry," Ed said, bringing cream cheese and tomatoes over to the counter. "I'm just worried about you, that's all."

"Yeah, I'd be worried about you, too, if you thought a knock on the door from Heather was actually triplet murderer ghosts coming to kill me."

"What?" Ed asked.

Jeez. Did I say that out loud?

Gaia was already getting used to this new expression on Ed's face. The one where he would squint and his head would shake ever so slightly as he searched Gaia's eyes, trying to gain a modicum of understanding. It was the face that said, "I'm sorry, *when* exactly did you become a raving lunatic?" "*Yesterday morning,*" she wanted to say. "*It started yesterday morning, Ed.*" But she said nothing. She wasn't about to attempt to explain everything her uncle had told her or done to her. It was almost too complicated for Gaia to understand, and Ed certainly didn't need to hear it.

Gaia just needed to find some way to control what was happening to her. Because if it was going to hurt Ed in any way, then she'd rather put herself in a nice rubber room now, get a walloping daily dose of Thorazine, and spend her days drooling with the rest of the psychopaths. Ed couldn't be damaged in any way, shape, or form. That was the only remaining rule in her life.

She looked up and locked eyes with Ed across the kitchen counter. "Ed. . . don't listen to me for a while, okay?" she murmured. "I'm not making a lot of sense right now, you know, from my fever and everything."

There was the look again. Ed's you've-gone-psycho glance. Even the request to ignore her insanity had come out sounding insane. But his eyes relaxed into a confident stare.

"Sure," he said. "I ignore most of the crap you say, anyway." Ed smiled at her as he bit into his bagel.

Had he always been this cute?

Yes. . . she supposed he had. But his morning cute. . . hair-even-more-of-a-mess-than-usual, collar-of-his-black-T-shirt-stretched-out-way-too-far-on-his-muscular neck morning cute. . . that was a whole new level of cuteness.

"What?" Ed asked, speaking with his mouth full as he froze midchew.

"What?" she asked defensively.

"What are you looking at?" he replied. "Are you seeing me with the head of a lizard or something?"

Gaia paused to give Ed the evil eye. Then she dug her hand into her bowl and created a Froot Loop ball that she successfully hurled in his face.

Ed let the Froot Loops cascade slowly down his cheeks. "I can't believe you just did that." He wiped his face clean.

"Yeah, well." Gaia smiled as she looked down at her bowl and began crunching on her breakfast again. "You may be cute, but you're still an asshole."

"*Aha!*" Ed bellowed, lunging across the table and pointing his finger in Gaia's face.

"What?" Gaia demanded.

"One of us just said I was cute," he said, as if he'd just proved the unified theory of physics. He leaned his face dangerously close to hers again. "And it wasn't me."

Gaia felt an electric current shoot down her spine

as he came toward her. She made no attempts to create additional distance between his lips and her own.

She wondered if perhaps she could just stay in this moment. The moment before a kiss. This moment cleared all the horrors from her mind and warmed her entire body, killing all the aches and pains. It was probably just her hallucinatory state, but Gaia still wasn't convinced that Ed didn't possess healing capabilities. His closeness seemed to reinfuse her with power. It was this purely electrical phenomenon. But it was just a little safer. As long as they were *before* the kiss, it was electricity that could be safely handled. Still no unwieldy shocks or dangerously high voltage that might be beyond her control.

That was the problem. If she moved to the next moment—the actual kiss moment—she wasn't sure she'd be able to control it anymore. If they reached that moment, she was rather sure that someone was going to end up getting shocked, big time. Electric-chair style.

But at this distance from his lips, it was pretty much beyond her control already. Sparks were already running up and down her back. And she wanted to move to that next moment. She really could no longer stop herself from moving to that next moment. . . .

But another knock at the door could stop them both.

Three hard raps to the front door turned both their heads and threw Ed back toward his stool. Gaia tried to regain her faculties after her brief journey from Earth to planet Ed.

Ed turned quickly to her, making sure she wasn't going to call 911 simply because someone was knocking at the door. She rolled her eyes and indicated with palms out that she was going to be cool this time. . . even though she was maybe a *little* troubled by the second round of knocking. Ed really didn't need to know that. She didn't want to give him any more evidence that she'd gone off the deep end.

"It's probably just Heather with coffee," he said, sounding mildly agitated. He grabbed his crutches and headed for the door.

"I'll come with you," she said, leaping off the stool to follow him. She hoped it had sounded nonchalant enough, even though the real plan was to sic herself on the Joshes she knew were standing behind that door.

Ed moved quickly, but Gaia managed to pass him and take the lead. She did her best to prepare herself for battle as she turned the knob and ripped open the door.

"Oh, thank God, you are okay!"

Natasha stepped into the room and wrapped her arms around Gaia before she could even move. Gaia wiggled her way out of the embrace. Disgust washed over her.

Natasha had somehow tracked Gaia down. And now she was standing in Ed's foyer, smiling with relief. Tatiana was only a few feet behind her, staring coldly from the hallway.

"What are you *doing* here?" Gaia hissed, once again seeing through Natasha's rigid fake smile. Gaia wondered if anyone had ever been foolish enough to think that sickly sweet look in her eyes was actually sincere. It was so clearly a sugarcoated facade, masking some other totally unknown identity. Gaia didn't want to think further on it. She just wanted her out of her sight.

"This is the question I should be asking *you*," Natasha stated, crossing her arms. Her anxiety had brought out her Russian accent even more. "You need to be home, Gaia, you know that. Your father has trusted me to take care of you. *Please* let me do that."

Gaia eyed Natasha's faux concern. "How did you even know I was here?" she asked suspiciously.

"Because the school office was kind enough to give me your best friend's address, that is how. And thank goodness they did, or I would still be at home, worried that you had gone out and gotten yourself *killed*. Please, Gaia, I beg you not to put me through this again. I need to know that I'm taking proper care of you. Your father needs to know this, too."

Gaia's eyes darted quickly to Ed's face—permanently confused, then to Tatiana's face—one hundred percent heartless resentment. Then she stared back into Natasha's eyes.

Maybe Natasha *was* sincere? But if that was true, then Gaia was beginning to realize just how much she'd been appreciating a parentless existence. The last thing she needed now was another fake authority figure who seemed to take on the substitute mommy role.

"You've got to be kidding me," Gaia breathed, crossing her own arms as she faced down Natasha. She asserted her power with a piercing stare. "I don't *know* you—I know the guy who hands me my chili dogs at Gray's Papaya better than I know you. The only person I know *less* than you. . . is *her*." Gaia pointed her finger directly toward Tatiana's too-elegant face.

Tatiana stared back in silence. Natasha's eyes drooped downward, as if Gaia's admonishment had deflated her entire body. "Well, that is why I have brought her here," she explained quietly. "So you can get to know her."

"Excuse me?" Gaia snorted.

"Tatiana is enrolled now at the Village School," Natasha said. "And whatever you may think of us right now, I. . . and she. . . were hoping that perhaps you might show Tatiana around the school today. To help her get acquainted."

Tatiana rolled her eyes and huffed. She turned to her side, looking disdainfully off into space.

Gaia couldn't believe her ears. "A buddy?" she asked, sneering at Natasha in disbelief. "You want me to be her *school buddy?*"

Tatiana bolted for the elevator.

"Tatiana!" her mother snapped. Gaia listened as Natasha scolded her quickly in Russian, forcing her to come back to the doorway and "try the way we've discussed." Tatiana obeyed her mother, turning around and marching robotically back to her first position.

"Please, Gaia?" Natasha asked. "My daughter has done nothing to you."

"Not yet," Gaia said, looking Tatiana over again.

Natasha stepped closer to Gaia, pleading with her eyes. "Gaia, we are family, you know. You and I... and Tatiana. We are all part of Katia's family. For *her*. For your mother. Be kind."

Gaia stepped closer as well, making sure she had the full attention of Natasha and her totally transparent, fluttering, big brown bullshit eyes. "*No,*" she said. "You don't talk to me about my mother. I don't know who you are, but you know what I do know? I *know* it's not who you say you are. And I want the two of you to stay out of my life, do you understand me? Because if you don't—"

"Gaia, come on." Ed grabbed Gaia's shoulder and pulled her away from Natasha.

"What are you doing?" Gaia snapped.

"Come on," Ed said, giggling uncomfortably to defuse the tension. "I mean, I don't even know what's going on here, but if this is just about showing her around school, I'm sure we can play nice here. *I'll* show you around," Ed said, shrugging at Tatiana.

Natasha grinned graciously at Ed. Tatiana dropped

her eyes shyly to the floor before peeking up at him. Gaia watched Ed smile back at her and felt a volcanic rumbling beginning in her stomach. *Uh-uh. No way. Nooo way.*

"That's okay, Ed," she said, shoving Ed back a foot and pasting a deeply ironic smile over her simmering rage. "You know what? I'd be more than *happy* to show Tatiana the ropes." *More like the gallows.*

"There, see?" Ed joked to Tatiana. "She's really a sweetheart once you get to know her."

"Oh, you bet I am," Gaia said, firing off imaginary poison darts at Tatiana with her smile.

"Then you'll do it?" Natasha asked.

"Oh, yeah, I'll do it," Gaia said, locking eyes with Tatiana. "Believe me, I will definitely do it."

"HE WAS SO BEAUTIFUL. DID I

So-called Lunch

mention how beautiful he was?"

Heather hadn't shut her mouth about Mr. Beautiful for the past twenty minutes, the VS cafeteria burrito tasted like dog poo in a gym sock, and if Tatiana laughed at one more of Ed's jokes without even knowing what the hell he was saying. . . someone

171

was going to die. It might have to be Gaia herself, but *someone* was going to die.

"Yes." Ed groaned. "I think you might have mentioned his beauty a few hundred times already."

"Well, he was," Heather said, leaning her face on her fist and twiddling two carrots on her plate. "He was like a Greek god."

"Yeah, with a lap full of coffee," Ed added.

"Exactly." Heather sighed wistfully. "And he was *so*—"

"Nice," Gaia interrupted, stabbing a fork through her so-called lunch. "He was so *nice*. We know."

"Did I mention that already?" Heather asked mindlessly.

"I think we caught that," Gaia muttered. Then she fell back into bitter silence, which had basically been her mode ever since they'd gotten to school. She divided her time between bitter silence and menacing stares at Tatiana, who was already shamelessly flirting with Ed. The only problem was, her silence kept forcing Ed to fill in the marathon pauses. He kept trying to keep the table talking, being the pathologically nice guy that he was. But every time he opened his mouth, he was talking to the same person. And it wasn't Gaia.

"So, Tatiana," Ed said, pulling her eyes up from her lunch—three pieces of lettuce. "Why did you and your mom come to America?"

"I would like to know this also," Tatiana said dourly, staring back down at her lettuce.

Another awkward pause. *Good,* Gaia thought. *I can't stand to listen to that wispy little voice again. I liked her so much more when she didn't talk.*

"Would you care to elaborate?" Ed pressed amiably. Tatiana let out a small, high-pitched giggle.

Stop flirting, Tatiana. Stop flirting or I swear to God. . .

Tatiana considered the question for another moment. "I think we are here because my mother thinks that this is land of opportunity, " she said. "But I say, opportunity for what? To listen to Britney's Spear?"

Ed and Heather cracked up.

"What?" Tatiana asked defensively.

"It's *Britney Spears.*" Heather giggled, like she was telling Tatiana a secret. "Not Britney's Spear."

"You see?" Tatiana said, flipping back her straight, flowing hair and throwing her elegant arms upward. "These are the things young people know in this country. They know of Britney's Spear and Christina Agamemnon, but do you know who is your secretary of agriculture?"

Ed and Heather went dead silent.

Ann M. Veneman. Does she think we're all idiots? Gaia could have said something, but she was opting not to speak.

"You see?" Tatiana said, her tone oozing with self-congratulation. "I rest in my case."

From dead silence to uproarious laughter again. *It's really not that funny,* Gaia was dying to tell them. Even Tatiana began to smile.

"What?" Tatiana said, giggling. "Should I not be resting in my case?" Soon she, too, was laughing. But she was never laughing with Heather. This was plain to see. Always with Ed. Only with Ed. Every single exchange at the table was addressed only to him.

The only person at the table not laughing was Gaia. She was too busy seething.

Stop. . . flirting. . . Tatiana.

Was she being paranoid? Was Ed just being "nice guy Ed," trying to bring Tatiana out, and Gaia had it all wrong? He was, after all, the only person who had been nice to Gaia her first day at this godforsaken school. . . .

No. No way. Gaia wasn't a paranoid person. She never had been. She never cared enough about what anyone else was thinking to be paranoid. She had legitimate reasons to be suspicious of Tatiana. Perhaps Ed could get her to *elaborate* on her little black book of notes she'd been taking on Gaia or the clever little ways she tended to hide from Gaia's view back in the girlie bedroom from hell?

"Come on, we have some good things to offer," Ed argued jokingly. "What about culture? Museums, opera, ballet. . . I bet you're a dancer, right? You look like a ballet dancer."

Gaia stared at Tatiana's ethereal, stick-thin body wrapped in formfitting Calvin Klein. Then she examined her own thick, muscular wrists. And then she looked back at Ed. *"I bet you're a dancer?"* Where'd you *learn that one, Ed?* The Frat Boy's Guide to Eastern European Flirting?

"I did do some dancing," Tatiana admitted coyly. "Among other things. . ."

Stop looking at him that way.

"Other things like what?" Ed asked.

Enough, Ed. Gaia could feel herself nearing eruption again.

"Oh, this is not important," Tatiana said, so obviously begging him to inquire further.

"No, come on," Ed said. "What else do you do?"

That'll do, Ed.

"No, you don't want to hear about this." Tatiana giggled.

"No, I *really* do," Ed insisted. "I'm *really* interested."

Tatiana tilted her head at Ed and smiled intimately. "You are so sweet—"

"*Enough!*" Gaia howled, throwing her fork down almost hard enough to crack the plate in half. She shot out of her chair.

Their mouths all dropped wide open. Along with the rest of the cafeteria kids'. Ed looked utterly dumbfounded. Heather actually looked scared. And Tatiana. . . Oh, who the hell cared how Tatiana looked? Gaia didn't care. She knew what was going on, and she wasn't going to put up with another second of it.

"Gaia. . . ?" Ed asked. "What the hell is—"

"Don't give me that *what's-wrong-with-you* act,

Ed!" She gave him a murderous glance. "Do you think I'm blind?" Gaia turned to Tatiana and leaned within striking distance. "And you—whatever you're trying to do, it won't work. I'm going to find out who you are. You and your mother. I'm going to find out the truth, and then we'll see how goddamn paranoid I am!"

Gaia slammed her chair against the table, rattling everyone's tray, then bolted through the rusty double doors of the cafeteria, nearly ripping them off the hinges. The entire third-floor hallway seemed to be rocking from side to side like an old-fashioned steamship. Maybe that was why everyone kept bumping into her, pummeling her like she was the wide receiver and they were all going for the tackle. She felt like she was covered in bruises by the time she made it to the stairs. Finally she popped through the school's front doors, where she could get some air.

But it didn't matter where she turned. Out here was no different than in there. They were still staring. Every one of them. What the hell was everybody staring at?

Gaia isn't Gaia—that's for sure. I can't even begin to understand it—her bizarre trans-formation. As far as I can tell, there could really only be one possible explanation.

Drugs. Gaia Moore is on drugs. Except. . . she's not. Gaia Moore doesn't do drugs. I'm quite sure of it. So what other explanation can there be?

And you want to know what's really scary? I shouldn't say this. I shouldn't even think it. But. . . I'm not altogether sure I don't like the transformation. I mean, sure, no one wants to be bitched out by a totally paranoid psychopath in the middle of the school cafeteria. But on the other side of that very ugly coin. . . Gaia was *jealous*. Demented, yes. Insane, no ques-tion. But still dementedly and insanely jealous.

Now, I'm sorry. I know this is probably not "psychologically correct" or whatever the term

might be, but am I the only one
who thinks that jealousy is an
indication of love? Okay, at
least major *like*? Well, okay,
infatuation, obsession, puppy-
loving stalker crush, that kind
of thing? I mean, her jealousy
was totally paranoid and based in
no reality whatsoever. I was just
working my ass off to make conversation. But still, there's a
legitimate compliment in there
somewhere, I think.

The thing is. . . . New Gaia
will be incredibly affectionate
and then ice-cold. She'll be near
tears and seemingly near death,
and then she'll sleep like a
baby. She'll be weirdly terrified. I've never seen her scared
in my life. And then she'll be
completely playful, and then
romantic, and then paranoid, and
then enraged. And she'll be all
these things in one twelve-hour
period. New Gaia is really nothing like Gaia at all. New Gaia is
like this. . . this. . . *totally
normal girl.*

She's human.

I don't know, I just think, whatever has happened to her. . . If this is the new Gaia, and if I can deal with her insane psychotic emotional explosions of rage. . . then I think I might love her even more now than I did before.

Have you ever read *The Catcher in the Rye*? What am I saying—of course you've read *The Catcher in the Rye*. Who hasn't read *The Catcher in the Rye*? Okay, here's my point: Could Holden Caulfield have been any more *right*? I don't care if he was coming to you from the mental ward; the guy was still dead-on.

Phonies. What a bunch of phonies people are. I don't know why I've never seen it as much as I do now. Since that injection. Something about that serum has just opened my eyes.

I sat there watching Tatiana work her whole little faux Princess Kournikova routine, and it just made me sick. All her coy giggles and those cleverly placed little malapropisms. She knew what she was doing every step of the way. Plotting and scheming. Preying on Ed's inherent kindness. Trying to divert his attention from me. Trying to rope him in, pitiful step by pitiful step.

I thought Heather was the master manipulator, but this girl's shtick makes Heather look like Snow White.

And do you know who she learned it from? Her mother, of course. Who else? That's where all these girls get their phony training. It's passed from generation to generation. Maybe that's why I'm so honest. I stopped training when I was twelve. Maybe if I'd had a mother for the last five years, I'd be a ruthless manipulator just like Tatiana and her mom.

No, I don't think so. Not with my mom.

And do you know what I noticed after I walked out of school? It's everywhere you turn. Everywhere. The second anyone opens their mouth, they're trying to get something from you, trying to pull one over on you.

School was out of the question, so I spent the rest of the day at Grand Central Station, conducting an anthropological study. And let me tell you, the problem was running rampant. Every human transaction was just a manipulation. A smile meant someone needed something. A laugh meant someone wanted something in return. Crying meant someone craved attention. The whole place was just a swarm of schemers.

One thing I know for sure—I don't want to be a part of any of it. That's why I have to get out of that apartment now. I'm packing what's left of my stuff, and I'm getting out of there tonight. Before those two schemers hold some kind of demonic séance over my bed and try to convert me while I'm sleeping. And believe me, they'd do it, too.

I'm on to you, ladies.

He found himself wishing that he had a spray bottle filled with water and some rubber gloves. **rewind** That always seemed to be what the experts used when the cat went crazy.

"WOULD YOU LIKE ANOTHER COOKIE, ED?"

Ed wasn't sure what Gaia's problem could possibly be with her new foster mom. Or Tatiana, for that matter. They seemed like two of the friend-

Devious Observations

liest, most generous people he'd met in a long time. And the digs weren't too shabby, either. The living room was about twice the size of Ed's, with freshly polished wood floors, brand-new white couches, long, flowing white curtains, and wide-open windows that looked down on posh East Seventy-second Street. What was Gaia doing, cramming herself into Ed's hospital bed when she could be stretching out on the Upper East Side?

He added that to the list of questions he would ask her if she ever actually came back to her new apartment. His other questions included such classics as: *Are you a paranoid schizophrenic?* And, *Are you in love with me?* Trivial things of that nature.

"Don't mind if I do," Ed said, smiling at Natasha as he handed her his plate for some more cookies. "They're unbelievable."

"Well, thank you," she said with a wide smile. "They are my grandmother's recipe. A highly guarded Russian secret." She winked at Ed and walked back to the kitchen, leaving Ed and Tatiana alone in the living room.

Ed could tell that Natasha was straining ever so slightly to keep things light. He'd heard how upset she'd gotten when he'd told her that Gaia had disappeared. She was obviously just as worried as he was.

It had turned into the mystery of the day. Where had she gone after her `paranoid freak-out` at school? Ed and Tatiana had formed something of an instant friendship ever since that moment—both victims of Gaia's drive-by irrational ambush. Tatiana had been kind enough to give Ed their number at home, but he'd called to check on Gaia's whereabouts so many times, he probably looked like something of a lunatic himself. He and Gaia truly were made for each other.

The incessant calling must have driven Tatiana and her mom so nuts that they'd finally invited him over so he could sit it out there. And so he and Tatiana had been chatting on the couch for the last hour now. Well. . . trying to chat. Tatiana's English still needed a little work.

"Ed," she said hesitantly, taking a pinch of cookie and meticulously placing it in her mouth. "I do not want to buzz into your life, but—"

"Butt," Ed corrected her.

"But?" she asked, tilting her head quizzically.

"Butt."

"But what?"

Ed breathed out a laugh. "No." He smiled. "It's *butt*, not buzz. You don't want to *butt* into my life. You don't buzz into someone's life. Well. . . Heather kind of buzzes into my life, but. . ."

"But what?" Now Tatiana looked deeply confused.

"No, that was it." Ed giggled, shaking his head apologetically.

Tatiana looked thoroughly perplexed at this point but still very determined to get it right. Ed probably wasn't helping. "So, Heather buzzes. . . but I butt?"

"Right, I mean, *no.*" Ed laughed. "I'm sure you're not butting in or buzzing in. What was your question?"

"I don't remember!" Tatiana laughed, slapping her hand dramatically to her head.

"I—"

"What the hell is going on here?"

Ed flinched. Gaia was standing on the top step of the sunken living room with her arms akimbo and a killer accusing stare. The moment Ed saw her face, he felt his lungs shrivel. If he'd had any hopes that her head might have cleared by now, he could forget it. Her face was tweaked. Her eyes darted back and forth between the two of them with a look that suggested murder was not out of the question.

Ed grabbed his crutches and hoisted himself out of his seat. "Where have you been?" he asked anxiously, walking toward her. "I've been going nuts. I didn't even hear you come in."

"Yeah, no kidding." Gaia snorted. "Where have *I*

been? I'd ask you the same question, but I see I don't need to. You're *exactly* where I left you, Ed. Laughing it up with my new evil stepsister." Gaia turned to Tatiana and took two menacing steps down toward her on the couch. "Hey, sis! How's the scheming going? Have you scored yet?"

Tatiana ducked her head and then peeked up at Ed, asking for help with her eyes. Probably something along the lines of, *Can you do something about your samurai best friend?*

"What is that look?" Gaia demanded. "A cry for help? Oh, now you're working the damsel-in-distress angle?"

Ed inched himself closer to Gaia, like she was a house cat that had gone wild. "Gaia, come on," he said with a cautious half smile. "She's just sitting there. She didn't do anything."

"Oh, excuse me, Prince Charming. I didn't mean to offend your fair lady."

Natasha bounded into the room, dropping the cookie plate on the dining table and rushing toward Gaia. "Oh, good, good." She sighed with relief as she approached her. "You're all right."

Gaia straight-armed Natasha, stepping back. "Ah, Wicked Stepmother's here, too!" she announced in a tone of ironic celebration. "And she's brought cookies! How delightful. Well, it seems like the family unit is functioning just fine without me, so I'll just grab a few things and then be on my way."

Ed swallowed hard and made his way toward her room. He found himself wishing that he had a spray bottle filled with water and some rubber gloves. That always seemed to be what the experts used when the cat went crazy. On second thought, this was Gaia he was dealing with. Perhaps a chair and a whip would be more appropriate.

When he entered her room, she was trying in vain to stuff a sweatshirt and a pair of jeans into a minuscule book bag. "Gaia. . . ?"

"Yup?" she snapped.

"Can I talk to you for a second?"

"Nope."

Ed stepped closer and leaned down. "Gaia, listen to me, okay? There's something wrong with you. I don't know what it is, but something's happened in your head, and I don't think it has anything to do with a fever."

"Don't start, Ed," she shot back at him as she whipped around. It was so lightning quick, Ed nearly fell back on his crutches. "I know what you're trying to do."

"What are you talking about?"

"You're trying to screw with my head," she said. "But it's not going to work, so just step back."

"Gaia, listen," he said, putting his hand on her shoulder gently. "Remember when you told me to ignore the crazy stuff coming out of your mouth? Well, I can't ignore this, okay? You have to talk to me.

You have to tell me what's going on because you're acting like a total crazy person. A total paranoid—"

"I'll tell you what's going on." She shook his hand from her shoulder, getting up in his face and glaring at him with a kind of mania that was beginning to make him extremely sad. "They're testing me, Ed," she announced, loud enough for them to hear. "That's what's going on here. They think I don't know, but I do. So if you want to be tested, then I hope you and the little princess have a lovely time."

"Gaia, what are you saying?" Natasha asked from the doorway. "Why are you saying these awful things about us?"

"I'm just trying to bring some truth into this house of phonies!" she shouted. "I think Ed deserves to know the truth about you and your little schemer skank of a daughter!"

"Gaia, that's enough!" Ed barked. "Listen to yourself."

"Just keep defending her, Ed," she shot back. "It's making me feel so much better." She began to back herself slowly toward Tatiana's bed. "You're so blind, Ed. She's got you totally snowed, can't you see that? If I'm so paranoid, then maybe she wants to explain *this*."

Gaia ducked over the side of Tatiana's bed and began rummaging through the things in her bedside drawer. "Where is it?" she muttered to herself. "Where the hell is it?"

"What are you doing?" Tatiana cried. "Stop that!" She bolted past Ed and lunged at Gaia.

"Aha!" Gaia exclaimed, shoving Tatiana lightly to the side and holding up a small black notebook. "Here we go. You want to know the truth about her, Ed? The truth is right here in this book." Gaia ripped it open and began flipping through the pages. "Maybe she'd like to explain all her copious notes and devious little observations. . . ."

Gaia suddenly went silent. Her face went blank. She looked through a few more pages of the black book slowly, and then she let it drop to the floor.

"Whatever," she mumbled. "I've had it with this place." She made her way to the door without even taking her bag, but Natasha did her best to block the doorway.

"I can't let you go again," Natasha insisted, holding her arm in Gaia's way. "You need to stay here, Gaia. Here is where it is safe, do you understand?"

"Safe?" Gaia scoffed. "Like I'm safe here with the two of you?"

"Why do you keep saying these things?" Tatiana finally shouted. "I have done *nothing* to you!"

"Nothing? You've done nothing to me? You've been here *two freaking days,* and you're already trying to steal my boyfriend!"

"I don't know what you are talking about," Tatiana breathed, looking stunned.

"Bull. Tell it to someone who's listening! I'm out of here." Gaia turned around, pushed herself by Natasha, and made her way to the door, leaving the three of them frozen in place. Two seconds later they all heard the front door slam shut.

Ed was momentarily stuck in a daze, desensitized by all the screaming and paranoid accusations. He leaned forward and swiped up the small black notebook from the floor. Sketches. The last few pages were filled with sketches. Beautifully detailed drawings of Gaia lying in bed.

"That is mine," Tatiana whimpered, grabbing the book out of Ed's hands. Ed looked for one brief second at Tatiana, and then he snapped out of his daze.

Wait a minute. Rewind.

Boyfriend? Did she just say "boyfriend"?

Ed didn't even remember getting down to the street. Had he said anything to Natasha or Tatiana before he left? Had he taken the elevator down or the stairs? His mind had discarded everything but the sight of Gaia's hair bobbing up and down as she ran down Seventy-second Street. And the word *boyfriend*. She was already three blocks ahead of him as she ran toward Central Park. That was where he needed to be now, and that was all he could think about.

When this whole nightmare was over, Ed was going to teach a course on running with crutches.

To: L
From: QR2

   Subject approaching Central Park via Seventy-second Street. Fifth Avenue entrance. Target is two blocks behind and closing. Please advise.

From: QR2
To: L

   Patience has been rewarded. These are optimal conditions for a more conclusive test. Target is unquestionably the one whom subject would fear losing most. This should yield the results we need. Attack the target. Once results are obtained, target may be terminated.

To: L
From: QR2

   Directives understood. Test results to follow.

Josh after Josh

SEVENTY-SECOND STREET WAS SO hideously sterile. Everything was so disgustingly clean. Where *was* she, anyway? What *was* the Upper East Side? Everything so tall, towering over her, utterly characterless. So monolithic and white, set against the black sky, trying to swallow her up, like miles of clean white latex stretching out before her, bending around her, caving in and squeaking under her feet as she ran. *Just keep running.*

Central Park was like a mass of wild green freedom waiting for her at the end of this cold stone grid of white boxes. Maybe if she got there, her mind would stop spinning. Maybe then she wouldn't have this grating feeling that someone or something was always behind her, just about to strike. Looming. That's what it was. The whole damn world was looming over her, like a dark cloud or a pile of falling rocks or a thunderstorm.

At least the park looked alive and not dead. At least there were places there where she couldn't be seen and she couldn't be followed. Where she couldn't hurt people and they couldn't hurt her.

Drawings. *They were just drawings, Gaia. Drawings of you. Not plots to destroy you. You just called a girl you don't even know a "schemer skank." You just called Ed Fargo your boyfriend. What are you doing? What the hell are you doing?*

No people. That was the only possible answer right now. She was doing just terribly with people. God willing, she'd stand a better chance with plants.

She ran through the smaller entrance to the park on Fifth Avenue, and then she cut right into the park. She didn't head down the main paths that led to the band shell and the fountain and the boat pond. Those were the more populated areas. Although at this hour it was mostly just joggers. Very stupid joggers. Still, she opted to head down a winding dirt path that led into a less landscaped area full of trees. Better chance of full human avoidance.

Wait a minute, she thought as her legs continued to move her forward. *Maybe this is a bad idea.* Washington Square Park, she knew. Central Park, she really didn't. Washington Square Park was about the size of maybe six city blocks combined. Central Park was about. . . eight hundred or so *acres.*

"Gaia!"

Ed's voice. *No, Ed, don't follow me. Don't be a fool. I'll rip your heart to pieces, and I won't even know why.* She increased her speed and cut into bushier and darker terrain.

"Gaia, will you give me a chance to catch up, please?" he yelled after her.

She picked up the pace, skipping over uneven slippery rocks she couldn't even see in the dark. Leaping over ditches, jumping over fallen branches, and ducking under leaves as they swiped her face and whipped against her shoulders. But she could still hear him closing in, panting desperately.

"Gaia, come on!"

Not now, Ed. Couldn't he understand that? Maybe in a little while. Maybe after she'd spent a couple of nights as a homeless lunatic in the park until she was picked up by city services and shipped to a mental hospital, where she could get at least twelve weeks of electroshock therapy or a good, solid lobotomy and then a few more weeks of behavior modification mixed with the proper medications and a not-so-strictly-Freudian therapist and a respectable job weaving baskets in a Zen Buddhist monastery. Maybe then Ed could give her a call.

"Man on crutches here!" he shouted after her between short breaths.

Leave it alone, Ed, please.

"Gaia! Man on crutches, you know what I'm saying? Man on crutches on hills and in bushes, slipping over rocks in the dark trying to talk to—*mmpf.*"

She heard a loud thud followed by the clacking of wood. And then a thick, eerie silence. She stopped in her tracks, listening to herself breathe.

"Ed?" she called behind her.

She heard nothing but the wind whistling through the trees, rustling the treetops in loud, gusty waves. There was some moonlight sifting in through the leaves and a little reflected light from the lampposts in the park, but it was dark. It was really dark now. *Come on. . .*

"Ed?" she called again, much louder.

Silence.

And the first hint of that not-so-pleasant feeling. The one she'd been learning more and more about every four to six hours. The sound of silence where there should have been the sound of Ed was doing very uncomfortable things to Gaia's chest and throat. Everything tightening. Everything closing, constricting. Sickening.

Gaia turned herself around slowly and began to walk, tracing with her memory which direction his voice had been coming from. "Ed, are you messing with me?" she called out, listening to her feet crunch the leaves as she searched for him blindly. No response. Only gusts of wind rumbling in her eardrums. She walked more quickly. "Ed, come on. Talk to me." Heart rate increasing. Stomach lurching. Breath shortening. "*Ed!*"

She cut through a patch of bushes into a clearing and nearly tripped. Her eyes shot down to her feet. A crutch. One of Ed's crutches. And beyond the crutch. . .

Ed's body. Blood trickling down his face from the side of his head.

Gaia stopped breathing. *Okay, disappear.* It had to be another hallucination. It had to be. She revisited every one of her horrific memories again right there in the center of that clearing where Ed's body lay. Her mother, clamping her hand to the side of her head as she cried. Mary's entire body thrust forward by the sharp knife sticking out of her stomach. Sam Moon on his knees, reaching out to her with gaping black holes in his chest... But they had all disappeared.

Ed's body wouldn't.

Disappear, Ed. "Disappear, Ed." Now she was saying it out loud, chanting it as her strained eyes stared down at him. She whispered it to herself again and again as she ran to his body and dropped down next to him on her knees. *This isn't happening. It's not happening.* But Ed's lifeless body wasn't going away. She placed her hand on his neck to feel for a pulse.

Still breathing. He was still breathing. Gaia's entire body heaved forward with relief. She lifted his head up off the ground and wiped the blood from the side of his face. "You're still breathing," she whispered between her own shallow breaths. "Don't you worry, Ed, you're still breathing."

"Hey, Gaia. Is he dead yet?"

Gaia's body froze. She turned her head back slowly, looking for the man who had just whispered to her. All she could see were trees—staring at her, reaching their contorted arms down to crush her.

"Josh?" she called out. "Stay away, Josh. Stay the hell away from him."

"It's us," she heard from her left.

"Yeah, you know. Us. The voices in your head," she

heard from the right. And then a raw, gravelly giggle from behind her.

"Stay away," she uttered from deep in her chest, swinging her head to all sides, trying to see past the darkness. "Don't come another step."

"But Gaia," he whispered. "How can we stay away? We're already in your head." Suddenly that voice was inches from her ear. She whipped her head around and saw a glint of his horrid smile before he smacked his fist down right in her face, knocking her over on her side. Two more of them came out of the bushes. Josh after Josh.

One of them grabbed Ed's body, dragging it from Gaia's side. "No!" she howled, lunging for his legs a beat too late. "Stay away from him!" she begged, jumping to her feet. "He hasn't done anything."

"Well, that's never the point, is it?" Josh said, walking toward her until his face was in clear view. He looked deep into her eyes and smiled. "You know we have to kill him now."

"*No.*" Gaia had grabbed Josh by his black shirt, bringing back her arm for a hard punch, when his counterpart grabbed her from behind, pinning her arm behind her back and raising a knife to her face. Gaia squirmed and shook to break loose, but the two of them worked together to restrain both her arms.

Now both her wrists were being held down, and there were two knives to her face. There was no move to be made as they dragged her toward the third Josh—the one who was now holding Ed's unconscious body.

"Gaia," he whispered, holding Ed's body up against his chest so that Ed's head was leaning back on his shoulder. "Check this out."

Josh reached behind his back and brought out a long steel knife. He turned to look at Ed and then brought the knife up to Ed's neck, pressing the blade as close as he could to Ed's jugular vein without making the cut yet. "I think I'm going to gut him. I'm just going to gut him from the top of his throat to the bottom of his stomach."

"Please," Gaia begged, shivering from futility and that hollow, painful, nauseating buzzing. "Please don't."

"But we knocked him out just to bring you back over here," Josh complained. "Just so you could watch him die. Come on, Gaia, it's only fair. Sam had to die. Why shouldn't *he?* Ooh, maybe it should be in the same spot where we did Sam. That would be more appropriate, maybe." Josh slid the knife down from Ed's neck and placed the tip right at the center of Ed's chest. "I think right in the heart, guys, what do you think?"

The other two nodded, gripping Gaia's wrists tightly.

"What do you think, Gaia?" he asked. "Are you scared yet?" Josh cocked the knife back and aimed for Ed's chest.

And all Gaia could do was watch. She would stand there and watch it happen. Watch Josh cut open the last person on this earth that she truly loved while she was held down by her own menacing hallucinations. How sick was that? She felt her entire body cave in as she stared at their knives, waving in her face. Everything was closing in on her again—the trees reaching down at her, the bushes climbing up at her, their cruel hands holding their knives and swirling around her in a blur like some `torturous carnival ride` as Josh pulled back for the kill. . . .

Wait.

Time almost seemed to stand still. Just for one moment. Just for one infinitesimal split second. But an entire novel's worth of revelations could take place in one split second.

Just wait. Slow it down for just one moment. It was something she had seen. A blip of vision that had struck her amidst all the chaos spinning around her.

Something about their knives. No. Not the knives themselves, but the hands *holding* the knives. Something tiny she had somehow missed on the hands of her sinister delusions. Tiny black letters tattooed on their inner wrists. . .

QR1 and QR2.

Those letters struck a chord in her. They sparked a memory. An image of a computer screen popped into her head. Something she'd witnessed on that Clofaze CD. Something about a *prototype*. And then a list of *qualified replicants. QR1—100% success. QR2—100% success,* and on and on down the list. . .

Put it together, Gaia. Put it all together. And put it together she did. In that one split second.

Of course. How could she have missed this?

Josh was the prototype. *Josh* was Loki's first specimen for his demented cloning experiment. And Gaia might be suffering from some nasty hallucinations lately, but these sinister delusions holding her hostage. . . they weren't delusions at all. They weren't nightmares come to life or ghosts who'd come to haunt her for her sins. They were nothing other than *qualified replicants*. Clones. They were Loki's goddamn test run. His early models. First editions. They were more of Loki's expendable pawns. Just like her.

And this revelation did something to Gaia. Something major. She could feel the physical and mental shift inside her. Realizing her nightmares were real. . . It was like waking up. Waking up from this extended bizarro dream state in which she'd been trapped for the last forty-eight hours. For the first time since her uncle had pricked her with that sedative, Gaia felt completely and truly awake. Able to tell reality from her own psycho fictions.

She'd thought that fighting off these Joshes was like trying to fight off her own madness, fighting off her own fears. But she wasn't trying to conquer her fears at all. She was simply trying to fight off another batch of Loki's goons. The same old thugs that she'd beaten down a thousand times before. They were just goons in Josh's clothing.

And just like that, her split second's worth of revelations was over. She watched Josh's knife coming down toward the center of Ed's chest, and she let go. Finally she could let it all go. And God, did she have a lot of repressed anger to express.

Step one: Total relaxation. It had finally returned to her body. Step two: Attack *now*.

With lightning agility she clamped her hands onto her captors' fists and used them as a counterbalance as she kicked her feet out at Josh.

"*Hai!*" she growled with deep release, kicking her left foot to Josh's knife and her right foot to his face. The knife flew from his hand as his head snapped back against the tree behind him, sending his whole body tumbling to the ground. Ed's body followed, landing a few feet to the right. Good. She'd tend to him in a second.

The moment her feet touched ground again, she rammed her knee into "QR2's" crotch, forcing him to release her so he could hug both his hands on his lower abdomen as he doubled over. This gave her the free hand she needed to grab "QR1's" arm with both hands and flip his ass to the ground.

"*Ugh*," he groaned as his lower back landed directly on a mossy rock jutting out from the dirt. Meanwhile Josh (or "QR3," perhaps—there was really no way of knowing) had risen back up from his tree collision, and he was coming hard at Gaia.

She flew into a quick somersault that brought her

up next to Ed's left crutch. Josh was charging toward her. She got a firm grip on the strong wooden crutch and sat completely still. *Wait for it. . . .*

At the exact moment he was upon her, she rose from the ground, twisting her body and swinging the crutch straight at his head like a long wooden bat. She leveled him with a crack to the back of the head that didn't sound unlike a bat hitting a baseball. Must have been his skull. He passed out cold on the ground. He and "QR1" were most definitely down for the count. But apparently "QR2" had managed to recover from his initial crotch injury.

He picked up his knife and charged straight for her. Why he would do that, she wasn't sure, but it was his loss. Gaia lanced him in the stomach with the rubber stopper of the crutch, causing him to double over yet again. Then she jabbed his foot with the crutch and swung it upward full force like a golf club, most certainly breaking his nose and sending his whole body hurtling backward to the ground.

And then there were none. It had taken no longer than fifteen seconds.

That was what she'd been so scared of? *That?* Of all the painful lessons she'd learned about fear thus far, this one was perhaps the most important to date: Fear was a waste of time.

Gaia would have liked to inflict more damage, but she had Ed to worry about right now. And that took precedence over vengeance. She ran back to Ed's side and lifted his head up in her hands—alive and breathing and not a ghost. She tapped on his face repeatedly, harder and harder—until he finally began to come to.

"What happened?" he croaked, looking up at her. "Someone hit me on the head. Hard." He brought his hand to the side of his head, where there was still some blood.

"Not too much happened," she said. "It was no big deal."

He tried to lift his head to see the carnage. Gaia gently pushed him back down.

"You know what?" she said. "You really don't need to see it. It'll only confuse you. Do you think you can get up?"

Ed nodded.

"Good," Gaia said. "Let's just go *that* way."

Gaia led Ed away in the opposite direction from the scene, supporting him all the way to Fifth Avenue. She helped hold him up on Fifth until she got them both safely in a cab back down to his house. Normally she would have passed out long before then. But she was quite sure she could wait until she got to Ed's to pass out. She had just awakened from a marathon nightmare, and she really had no desire to go right back to sleep.

To: L
From: J

    Test complete. Subject has proved fearless under the most extreme of circumstances. Operated at 100% skill level. Results are conclusive.

To: J
From: L

    Excellent. We can proceed with phase II of the experiment. QRs to the MedLab. Proceed immediately to your next mission.

She had been
wearing her
id on her **raving**
sleeve for **lunatic**
two
straight
days.

HOW COULD HE POSSIBLY NOT BE

Gorgeous Dent

asleep? After completing a full-scale Crutch Olympics obstacle course in Central Park and receiving a bash to the head that had earned him a bump the size of a small ant farm, Ed had figured he would probably sleep for the next three to five business days. God knows he'd passed out hard enough when they finally got home. So what was he doing up at four-twenty-two in the morning? But whatever the reason, when he turned over on his side, he was glad he had awoken or he would have missed it. He would have missed the chance to see Gaia's face bathed in stripes of blue moonlight and white streetlight as she slept peacefully next to him in bed—the key word being *peacefully*.

Ed had no idea what had happened. But somewhere between his being clocked on the head and his coming to—a period of time that couldn't have been much more than five to seven minutes—Gaia must have found herself a good shrink and had the most incredible therapy session of her life. Either that or she'd gotten herself off the drugs. Because at least for now, Gaia seemed to have sent her paranoid insanity off for a long vacation.

Ed watched her sleeping for a while until he could no longer resist touching the beautiful image. Surely she would sleep right through it at this point, anyway.

Slowly and as gently as possible, Ed reached his hand over to her face, placed his fingertips at the top of her powerful jaw, and ran his fingers along her cheek, stopping at that `gorgeous dent` just behind the bottom of her ear.

Gaia suddenly began to shift her head on the pillow. *Oh, crap. She's awake.*

Ed's reflex reaction was to snap his hand away, slam his eyes shut, and fake a very sound sleep. He included a light fake snoring. That always did the trick.

"ED. THAT'S THE LAMEST FAKE

snoring I've ever heard."

Gaia raised her head up in the bed to get a better look at him. He opened his eyes and turned back to her. "What are you talking about? That's brilliant fake snoring."

Comfortable Silences

"You sound like a goat clearing his throat."

"Yeah, well. . ."

Gaia examined the bump on his head, touching her index finger gently to the bruise. "Does it hurt?"

"It kills," he said.

"I'll go get you some ice." Gaia got one foot off the side of the bed before Ed grasped her arm.

"Don't go," he said quietly. "Stay here, okay?"

She stopped herself and pulled her foot back onto the bed, looking deep into his eyes. And all she could think of, watching the expression on his face, was how jealous she was. Jealous of his ability to simply state what he wanted and how he felt without the slightest concern for how it would come out, what it might sound like, what it might mean. She wished he could give her some pointers right now. Because there were things Gaia wanted to say to him now, and she had absolutely no clue how to say them.

"I'm staying," she replied, laying her head back down on the pillow as she mentally skated over Ed's profile.

"Gaia," he said, turning on his side so they were face-to-face in the bed.

"Uh-huh."

"Do you want to tell me what happened to you?" he asked. "Because the last time I saw you, you were. . . how should I say this. . . a raving lunatic. And now you seem to be you again. Maybe even sweeter than you before you stopped being you."

Gaia had no idea how to even begin to answer Ed's question. Nor could she be at all sure she'd seen the last of raving lunatic

Gaia. For all she knew, she'd pop right back up the next time there was a knock at the door.

To answer his question fully, things would have to come out of her mouth that would surely convince him that her insanity was far from gone. *Well, see, I got this injection. . . blah, blah, blah. . . and it turned out the three Joshes were real! See?* No. That wasn't going to work.

And then there was also the fact that Gaia didn't really know the answer to his question. She'd experienced a whole slew of horrific emotional and psychological blitzkriegs that still made absolutely no sense to her. After all was said and done, it was possible that the only real way to describe it was that whatever was happening to her, for whatever reasons, just seemed to sort of. . . wear off. Spurred on by a couple of key revelations. What she said to Ed was even less helpful.

"I think that I forgot who I was for a while. . . and then I remembered."

Ed stared at her blankly. "Uh-huh."

"Yeah." She sighed. "Sorry. I suck at explanations."

"That's okay," he said.

They shared one of their newly established comfortable silences. But Gaia could tell that Ed had another question. Could he tell that she had something she wanted to say? Probably not. As she had already established for herself, she sucked at that, too. It seemed relationships tended to draw attention to the things one sucked at.

"Gaia. . ."

"Yeees?" she said, laughing at his slow delivery.

"Do you happen to remember back when you were a raving lunatic. . . the last thing you said. . . about—"

"No," Gaia interrupted him. "What's weird. . . is that I really don't remember much of what I said at all." That was a full frontal lie. She remembered the "boyfriend" blurt-out all too well, but it was simply too embarrassing.

"I see," Ed said. He didn't discuss it any further.

Ugh. She was still having massive trouble chalking up any honesty points here. Gaia wondered how many more things she would say that were the absolute opposite of what she was *trying* to say.

What she had slowly begun to realize was that raving lunatic Gaia had certain advantages that regular Gaia didn't. She had been wearing her id on her sleeve for two straight days. And while a lot of that id was chock-full of freak-outs and paranoia, the thing was. . . whenever she was alone with Ed, it was also chock-full of. . . that other thing. The thing she was trying to say to Ed.

But maybe that was the problem. She was trying to *say* things. Raving lunatic Gaia tended to act first and talk later. Maybe that was the key lesson. Gaia would never be able to wrap her mind around her feelings for Ed. They were too complicated. Too hard to dissect. The words would never come out right. She needed to act first and let her mind follow. Like the true raving lunatic she was.

Without another word spoken, Gaia simply placed her body back in the last intimate position she remembered them sharing. She quickly shimmied toward him until the tip of her nose moved past the tip of his and their chins were nearly touching. Ed's eyes widened.

Her psycho persona had gotten her this far. Maybe she could take it from here. Maybe she was brave enough now. The good thing about four-thirty in the morning was that there would be no knock at the door this time. This time Gaia was determined to get to that next moment, no matter how the hell she needed to get there.

Okay. You're in position. Ed thinks you've lost your mind again, but at least you're in position. Now talk. *Say something. Anything. Say whatever's on your mind. Jesus. . . what is on your mind?*

"Sometimes. . . I lie to you, Ed," she said. That's what was on her mind. *You idiot. Great opening line. First thing a guy wants to know is what a liar you are. Keep talking.* Her lips were nearly touching his with every word. Their eyes were so close, it was hard to pick which one to focus on. Especially in this dark blue light.

"You do?"

"I do," she said. At least it was the truth. At least now she was telling him the truth here in the dark, feeling his breath against her cheek. Was it the dark that was making her honest or just being this close to him? "I think I've been lying a lot," she went on. "Like when I tell you I don't remember saying. . . things. . . when I remember every single word I've said."

"That was a lie?"

"Yes," she confirmed.

"But why?" Ed asked. "Why do you lie?"

"Because I suck at this, Ed."

"At what?"

"At *love*, Ed," she admitted. "I suck at love." With that she let her lips fall against his with a kiss that fired the warmest, most gorgeous blue electricity down her spine and through to the tips of her once aching toes.

And nothing hurt anymore.

She ran her hand across his stubbly face and his firm shoulder through to the back of his neck. She felt his hand press against the small of her back as he kissed her. His kiss had all those same qualities that she envied so much. It had no guile or inhibition, just the purest, most unrelenting expression of wanting her—of how much he wanted her.

And somehow she had finally done it. Just like that, she had let herself love him.

HEATHER HAD NEVER IN HER LIFE

stooped this low. Men had been knocking down her door for dates as far back as she could remember, but here she was. . .

One-Two Punch

Staking out Starbucks. Waiting for Mr. Beautiful.

Shame, Heather. Shame on you. You shall never speak of this night to the Gannis family or to any of your admiring friends, who know full well that you could have the date of your choice at any given moment of your choosing.

It was true. With the exception of one Edward Fargo, Heather was quite sure she could get a date quite easily without resorting to manipulative stalker rituals that required loading up on lattes and double espressos. It just so happened that Heather did *not* have a date lined up for tonight or. . . for the rest of the year, and she wasn't at all ashamed to admit that she had developed something of a. . . fixation. Though in her defense she would ask this: Who would *not* develop a fixation when introduced to the most beautiful man in the world? Who would be that strong?

Certainly not Heather.

And certainly there was nothing *desperate* or *lame* about committing a few solid hours to that fixation. Though five hours might be pushing it.

Five hours. Five hours' worth of overheard inane

conversations. Five hours' worth of *InStyle* magazine. Five hours' worth of hair and makeup checks. And most important—that was to say disturbingly—five hours' worth of caffeine. Heather's heel had been tapping out extensive Morse code messages for a while now.

And so of course, ultimately she respected that one couldn't expect to have the luck of spilling boiling hot coffee in the lap of the same person twice. It wasn't natural. So finally Heather had packed up her trusty minibackpack and headed for the door. She had obviously wasted her time.

But halfway to the door she nearly twisted herself into a large, human-size pretzel.

Holy Mother of Mercy.

He had returned. Defying all common laws of chance and dating, Mr. Beautiful had returned to Starbucks—*this* Starbucks—*tonight*. The one night Heather had decided a stakeout was in order.

Now, that's destiny. I'm sorry, but may the big man upstairs strike me blind if that right there is not destiny.

So her five hours of overcaffeination had proved a worthwhile sacrifice. He was back, and she was ready for him. Now she just needed to look like she didn't care.

Heather quickly crammed herself into a visible table and slapped open the *InStyle Magazine* again, grabbing an empty cup of coffee from the windowsill and pretending to drink from it.

And in five, four, three, two...

"Well, look who's decided to show her face again at Starbucks," he joked, standing at her table.

Heather looked up, threw him a little of the I-have-a-faint-recollection-of-you eyes, followed by the gasp into hand over mouth. "Oh my God," she exclaimed. "I didn't even recognize you!" God, he was beautiful!

"Without coffee all over my pants, right?"

"Oh. Right."

"Can I sit down?"

Place ounce of hesitation here and...

"Oh, *sure*, sure."

He sat down across from her, and she quickly rested her chin on her fist. Otherwise she feared her jaw might drop wide open. Most men with the actual title of Mr. Beautiful couldn't possibly be as beautiful on the second viewing. He was *more*. Last time he'd gone with "clean-cut, just back from the gym," but this time he was going with "disheveled and sexy." The two looks in succession were the ultimate one-two punch.

"Do you want some coffee?" he asked.

"I'd love some!" she lied. "I'll get it." She shot out of her seat.

"No, no, I'll—"

"Oh, come on," Heather interrupted. "It's the least I can do."

"Okay," he said. "Coffee, black, please. Just be sure not to spill it on anyone."

"Very funny," she said dryly. She tapped him on the back of the head.

"*Ow,*" he groaned, pulling his head away.

She stared at him in surprise. "Did I hurt you?"

"No, no," he said. "Just bumped my head in the shower this morning, that's all."

"Oh, you poor thing," Heather said, flashing her best puppy dog eyes. "Well, I'll be right back with the coffee."

Heather ordered herself a hot chocolate and his coffee and got herself back to their table as quickly as possible. She didn't want to lose any momentum. The moment she sat down, she started to stare again. That jet black hair, mixed with those Superman blue eyes. And that smile. That amazing smile.

"Here you go. . . . Oh, you know what?"

"What?" he asked.

"You know, I can't believe this," Heather said with an embarrassed giggle. "I don't even know your *name*. How horrible is that?"

"It's not horrible at all," he said, putting out his hand. "Josh."

Heather shook his hand officially. "Well, I'm very pleased to meet you, Josh," she said.

"Likewise," he said.

Josh. She loved it. So manly and concise. Rolled right off the tongue. *Josh.* It was the perfect name for the perfect guy.

here is a
sneak peek of
Fearless™ #20:
SEX

His
lips. . .
what was it   **28**
about **minutes**
his lips?

Shivers

"DO YOU WANT ME TO CLOSE THE window?"

Ed had pulled his lips away from Gaia's and brought his head back just far enough to look her in the eyes. His hair was still hanging down on her forehead, keeping them connected, as he smiled at her with the most Ed-specific guileless adoration.

"Why?" Gaia whispered, doing her best to breathe regularly in spite of the fact that her heart was beating triplets.

"Aren't you freezing?" he whispered sweetly. "You're shivering like crazy."

Gaia froze from sheer embarrassment though she was not the least bit cold. Her eyes froze over as well, with a momentary attack of deer-in-headlights syndrome. "Oh. . . yeah," she stammered. "The window. Good idea."

Ed reached over Gaia in the bed and dragged his bedroom window shut, cutting off what was left of the city street noise at five in the morning.

She actually would have much preferred to keep it open, but what was she supposed to say? Was she supposed to tell him the truth? That she was shivering from his kisses, and his soft lips on her neck, and the feeling of his palms and his fingertips running along her waist? That the shivering was some kind of involuntary physical manifestation of how inconceivably happy she was at this moment, on his bed, in his arms, in the abnormally bright mix of ocean-blue moonlight and stark white New York streetlight?

No. That was unquestionably something to be felt and not to be said. Like a million other things she was feeling now, staring back into his eyes.

The brief window exchange had finally pulled their lips and bodies apart after twenty-eight minutes, and Ed leaned back to his pillow, running his finger along Gaia's cheek.

Just twenty-eight minutes. Gaia couldn't believe it. Twenty-eight minutes since she'd confessed—at least, in her own way—that she loved him. How could this version of them be only a half hour old?

But that really wasn't true, was it. Not if Gaia wanted to be completely honest with herself. Not if she wanted to dig past the paper-thin labels and relationship rules set up by the pre-*When Harry Met Sally* generation. The fact was, that movie was not just for liberal Upper West Side yuppie men and women over thirty. In truth, if all seventeen-year-olds could speak as honestly as Harry Burns and Sally Albright, then they too would have to confess that there was probably *something* else going on under their "best friendships" with members of the opposite sex.

"Friends" may have been the label for Gaia and Ed, but given the particularly honest mood she was in at this moment, Gaia had to admit that in some way, she and Ed had sort of been "courting" for the last year. In spite of all the love and tragedies they'd experienced apart from each other. In spite of a million other things, Gaia and Ed were a constant.

Maybe that was why, once she'd admitted what she was feeling, it was suddenly so easy to be so close. Almost as if they'd been together this way the entire time. Twenty-eight minutes into this relationship, and Gaia had found herself with a boyfriend whom she knew inside and out and trusted even more than she did herself.

Ed cocked his head to the side and searched Gaia's eyes with a mildly bemused smile. "What are you thinking?"

"Nothing," Gaia responded instantly. Man, did she need to work on the spoken honesty thing.

"You're still working on the spoken honesty thing, aren't you," Ed said. *God, he's good.*

"*No,*" Gaia squirmed. "I just. . ." *Oh, Gaia, cut it out. You've got nothing left to hide now.* "Yeah," she admitted. "Yeah, I'm having a little trouble in that category."

"Okay," Ed said purposefully, jamming his elbow into his pillow and leaning his head on his hand, "let's do a little exercise in honesty, then—"

"Oh, hell no," Gaia interrupted.

"Come on," Ed laughed. "It's five in the morning. Who's going to know? What, are you afraid?"

Oh, he didn't want to go there. *Gaia* didn't want to go there. That was the question of the hour. *The* question. Was her uncle's injection a phony or not? Was fear now a part of her life or was that all a hoax? Was her fearlessness genetic, or part of some governmental excuse for a science project put together by her father and a bunch of freakazoid CIA doctors? No, sir, she would not be going there. Not on this beautiful dark morning in this safe bed with her glorious new "everything" looking into her eyes. Whether she was now capable of fear or not, in this bed, with this boy, she was not afraid of anything.

"No," Gaia assured him. "I am most definitely not afraid."

"Fine, then you just have to answer a few questions honestly."

"Fine."

"Fine. Okay. Question one: Do you find me. . . *attractive?*"

"Okay, I quit," Gaia said, turning towards the window.

"Kidding," Ed laughed, pulling her back towards him.

"You've got one more shot," she said, with a comical glare.

"Okay," Ed agreed, staring into her eyes again. He shifted onto his stomach and moved closer until their noses were nearly touching. But he really shouldn't have done that. Not if the goal was to have a conversation. It had already been established in the last twenty-four hours that when the two of them got this close, talking was not the first inclination. "Okay. . ." he began again. "All right. . ." Ed seemed unable to produce a full sentence as his eyes had refocused on Gaia's mouth. "Okay. . ."

His mouth was so close to hers, she could feel the consonants rolling off of his lips. And the shivers had started again. First lightly in her toes. Then sudden heavy trembles in her stomach. His lips. . . what was it about his lips? Before she could answer her own question, she'd found that her hand had drifted up to his mouth to investigate. Without any specific orders from her brain, her fingers had begun to gently trace down from his lips to the corner of his mouth.

"Um," he uttered, inching his face closer. "Do you. . ."

"What. . . ?" she whispered, doing her best to cover the shivers.

Ed seemed utterly dazed by her fingers. "Do you want—"

"Yes." Gaia pressed her lips against his, channeling all the pent up energy of her trembling into her kiss. Ed responded with equal force, wrapping his hands tightly around her waist. But Gaia's T-shirt had ridden up slightly when he grabbed her, leaving Ed's wide palms suddenly pressed against her bare back. This sent another bolt of electricity up her spine that in no way helped to calm her shivers.

Ed's shirt had also apparently hiked up slightly, and when Gaia's hands drifted down to his waist to hold him, her fingers ended up grazing along the bottom of his exposed abs, sliding up along his muscular back and clinging to his bare shoulders under his shirt. It may have been an accident but it only led to higher voltage trembling.

And with her lips on his lips, and their hands clinging to each other's backs, Gaia slowly began to realize that the moment when her brain or her body would bring things to a halt did not seem to be coming. She didn't want to stop. There was no reason to stop. Not when she loved him this much. Not after building a year's worth of totally untainted trust. All she wanted now was to be closer to him. As close as was humanly possible.

Her hands on his bare back did not have to be an accident. Not if she didn't want it to be. So she simply let her hands follow through. Without rushing or tugging, Gaia let her arms continue to slide upward, lifting Ed's T-shirt higher and higher off of his chest, until he'd raised his arms and let her pull the T-shirt off.

She slid her hands across his bare shoulders and kissed him again as he returned his palms to the exposed small of her back. Now she could feel just how quickly his heart was beating.

But Ed pulled back momentarily, bringing his hands up to Gaia's face and giving her a kind but penetrating stare. "Gaia," he said between increasingly rapid breaths. "Are we about to do what I think we're about to do?"

ONE CRISP SUN-DRENCHED MORNING,

Murderously Gorgeous

two grande lattes, and Josh Brown. There could be no finer combination. At least not as far as Heather was concerned.

It was what Heather liked to refer to as a "*Mary Poppins* morning." One of those mornings where the spirit of Walt Disney had not just taken over Times Square, but all of New York City, even below Fourteenth Street and down to the Astor Place Starbucks. The trees seemed to be politely stepping out of their way for her. All the ruffled unshaven bohemians seemed to lock arms and dance a two-step down lower Broadway, while cartoon birds seemed to flitter down from the bright blue sky and perch on Heather's finger, winking at her and exchanging whistled melodies as she hovered her way into Starbucks.

Of course none of the above had taken place, but something far more dreamy and miraculous had: Josh's unheard of and all-too-daring *Morning Follow-up*.

Heather still couldn't believe it. She and Josh hadn't finished their last coffee rendezvous until midnight last night. But at the end of that unbelievable evening, Josh had actually suggested that they meet again *the very next morning*. Nine hours. Nine hours between coffee dates. That kind of dating proximity was generally reserved for either deep insatiable love affairs or desperately lonely people. And considering Josh's inhumanly beautiful appearance, loneliness was simply not a possibility. *Not* that Heather thought he'd developed a deep insatiable love for her after one spilled coffee encounter and one semi-impromptu Starbucks chat. But nine hours? Even Romeo could wait more than nine hours to see Juliet. Things were looking awfully good.

And Josh was looking awfully good. His black T-shirt left no distractions from his perfectly sculpted angular face and arms, and his slightly spiky, still-wet-from-the-shower jet-black hair.

"You have got to be kidding me," he said, ducking

his head down in disbelief after Heather sat down at their sun-warmed window table.

"What?" she asked, widening her eyes with concern. Had she done something wrong before she'd even sat down?

Josh brought his head back up and stared at Heather, his eyes reflecting in the sun like blinding purple neon. "You can't look this good at nine in the morning," he said. "No one looks this good at nine in the morning."

"Oh," Heather smiled, feeling her feet melting into her Clergerie shoes. "Well, I. . . ." She could do nothing other than smile and look like an idiot. Was there any possible response to that? Probably there was, but not when Josh said it there wasn't.

"You're one of *those*, aren't you?" he said.

"One of what?" she replied shyly.

Josh leaned forward on the table. "You're one of those girls who looks equally as beautiful when she gets out of bed in the morning as she does on a Friday night at seven-thirty."

"Okay, *stop*," she giggled, averting her eyes from his murderously gorgeous grin. She silently prayed that he would not stop.

"No, really," he went on. Her prayers had been yielding unprecedented success these last twelve hours. First he'd shown up at Starbucks last night after her wishful semi-stalker-like stakeout. Then came his suggestion of Morning Follow-up coffee. And now this. "Really. I bet you look like this the second you climb out of bed."

Now her legs had pretty much melted as well. When Josh said the word "bed," Heather found it somewhat difficult to breathe, let alone put together a verbal response.

"I'm sorry," Josh said with an embarrassed chuckle as he leaned back in his chair. "Did that just come out ludicrously inappropriate? I didn't mean—"

"No, it's fine," she assured him with a nervous laugh. "It's just not true, believe me. I'm sure you look a hell of a lot better than I do in the morning."

Was that the right response? *Stay cool, Heather, you're losing your touch here.* Heather considered herself to have something of a Ph.D. in Flirtation, but Josh made it next to impossible for her to keep her feet planted on the ground. Perhaps that had something to do with the fact that he'd already melted her feet. And her legs for that matter.

"Look, I'm sorry," he complained, shaking his head. Heather had no idea what he was sorry about, but she immediately felt her heart droop down into her stomach. Good Lord, this was bad.

"What?" she uttered, trying to mask her concern.

"I'm sorry, I just have to ask. . ."

"Ask *what?*" she whined inadvertently.

"Okay," he said, planting his elbows on the table with a confrontational glance. "When I found you here last night. . ."

Oh, God. Busted. Totally busted. Heather grabbed her lukewarm latte and guzzled half of it down, looking for a calming jolt of caffeine. He knew she'd been waiting for him. He must have known that she'd been on a five-hour stakeout for him. She might as well have had a huge pair of binoculars hanging around her neck, a pith helmet, and a group of resentful natives carrying her supplies. She'd fallen down into the ranks of the hunter-explorer girls. The millions of non-self-respecting `stalker-skanks` across the nation who lived for no other purpose than to entrap some unsuspecting *dude* and seduce their way into "last resort late night hook-up" status with him.

"I just don't understand," Josh went on as Heather cringed internally. *Go on. Say it. Just say it.* "I don't understand what a beautiful girl like you could have possibly been doing alone at Starbucks last night."

Heather's head suddenly felt much lighter. Another compliment. Not the end of line. Could she be any more sensitive? Any more of a full-blown loser? *Relax, girl. You're Heather Gannis for God's sake. Never to be confused with the pathetic Hunter Skanks of the world.*

She tried to shake off her panic as quickly as possible, hoping it hadn't shown through her long-rehearsed emergency smile.

"Come on, tell me the truth," he said with a sly grin. "Did you *just* break up with your boyfriend or something?"

She was so relieved to be undiscovered that she didn't even bother holding back with her answer. "Well, not exactly, *just*," she said, without even thinking. She guzzled some more latte to ease her sudden dry mouth. "It was a little while ago, but, *after* we broke up. . . he kind of moved on to this other girl I know."

Ugh. That was unpleasant to say out loud. Did Josh really need to know this?

"Ooh," Josh groaned with a comic wince. "Were you, like, good friends with this other girl?"

"No," Heather laughed, looking more and more at her coffee. "Far from it."

She found herself wondering what Ed and Gaia were doing at this very moment. The last time she'd seen them, Gaia had actually gone pretty much berserk in the cafeteria, spewing out a totally uncharacteristic jealous tirade at Ed and her new Russian roommate (or something) Tatiana.

Watching them fight could have been some kind of weird relief for Heather, as in maybe things weren't so damn heavenly in the world of Ed and Gaia. But the fact was, watching Gaia go nuts on Ed and Tatiana had only made Heather feel worse. Jealousy. It was the ultimate proof Heather needed. If she'd had any doubts, now she knew for sure that Gaia was in love with Ed. Only love can make a girl go off on someone like that.

So what were they doing at this moment? They'd probably made up already. And two people are never more in love than when they make up after a fight. They make up. And then they have the makeup hug. And then the makeup kissing.

And then the make up sex.

That's probably what they were doing at this moment. Having wild passionate makeup sex. Whatever. *Whatever. She doesn't deserve him. She doesn't deserve to know what it feels like to be with him. I was his* first. *There's nothing anyone can do to change—*

Whoa, Heather. New leaf! Where the hell is your new leaf?

Right. The new leaf that Heather had worked so hard to turn over. She was through with resentment, and selfish thinking, and petty jealousy. New Heather didn't have those feelings. New Heather was Gaia's friend. New Heather tried to help Gaia out of a jam when she needed it. New Heather just wanted to see Ed happy—whomever he was with. Right? Yes. . . . Yes, that's right.

"Heather?"

"Huh?" Heather looked back up at Josh. His expression seemed to suggest that he was waiting on an answer to a question. Though Heather hadn't heard a thing.

"I said are you jealous? You know, of this girl who stole your *man*," he joked.

Heather tried to answer before allowing herself to think further. "No," she blurted out. "I'm not. . . I mean. . . I'm really trying to stay away from that kind of thinking, you know. . . petty jealousies and stuff like that."

Josh's grin grew wider as he leaned his stunning eyes closer to Heather's. "Come on," he crooned, searching deeper with an extremely cute little taunting glint in his eye. "It's not petty, Heather, it's *human*. You don't have to pretend with me, you know. You hardly know me. And I don't know them. It's the perfect situation to confess. *Confess*, Heather," he joked, pointing his finger directly in her face with the archetypal glare of the Grand Inquisitor. "Thou wilt confess thy jealousy."

Heather could not help but laugh. Gorgeous, smart, and funny. She would think he was just a dream if his long thick finger were not pointing directly between her eyes.

"Well. . ." she began with a half smile. "I did kind of used to. . . *despise* the girl."

"Ahhh," Josh exclaimed with a satisfied grin. He

ran his finger down the center of Heather's nose, inducing a full body tingle the size of Canada. "A little honesty. That's more like it." He leaned towards her. "Okay, Heather," he said with the mock seriousness of a Freudian psychotherapist. "This mystery girl. Let's discuss your hatred of this mystery girl. I think it would be very good for you."